First Love

Also by Gwendoline Riley

My Phantoms

First Love

GWENDOLINE RILEY

nyrb **New York Review Books** New York

This is a New York Review Book

published by The New York Review of Books

435 Hudson Street, New York, NY 10014

www.nyrb.com

First published in Great Britain by Granta Books, 2017

LIBRARY OF CONGRESS CATALOGING-IN-PUBLICATION DATA
Names: Riley, Gwendoline, 1979– author.
Title: First love / By Gwendoline Riley.
Description: New York : New York Review Books, [2022] | Series: New
  York Review Books Classics
Identifiers: LCCN 2022001037 (print) | LCCN 2022001038 (ebook) |
  ISBN 9781681376905 (paperback) | ISBN 9781681376912 (ebook)
Classification: LCC PR6118.I43 F57 2022 (print) | LCC PR6118.I43
  (ebook) | DDC 823/.92—dc23
LC record available at https://lccn.loc.gov/2022001037
LC ebook record available at https://lccn.loc.gov/2022001038

ISBN 978-1-68137-690-5
Available as an electronic book; 978-1-68137-691-2

Printed in the United States of America on acid-free paper

10 9 8 7 6 5 4 3 2 1

I

1

I used to look at houses like this one from the train: behind the ivy-covered embankment, their London brick, sash windows. That was on the Euston approach. The back of this flat – that is, the bedroom, the bathroom and Edwyn's study – looks out on the overground line, just past West Brompton.

I've been here for eighteen months but my boxes only recently came out of storage. Also in the consignment was my metal document case, half-full of old papers, correspondence, a few photographs. I spent a long afternoon unpacking onto the new alcove shelves, deciding what to keep.

When I first moved in, and before that, when I came to visit (I think I came three times), I'd watch for Edwyn in the evenings: standing between the windows, eyeing the shadows out there. This is a short, curved terrace. Mullions and porch columns rib the way. The traffic might build at night but the pavements are never busy; the procession was thin down from Earl's Court, until at last there he'd be: blond hair poking from a black flat cap, grey overcoat flapping, his tatty rucksack on one shoulder. In his free hand he always held a bottle by the neck, wrapped tightly in its striped plastic bag.

Lately it's the round of coughing in the hallway that lets me know he's home. I go out and meet him, we have a cuddle, and then I look at the *Standard* while he gets changed. We don't talk much in the evenings, but we're very affectionate. When we cuddle on the landing, and later in the kitchen, I make little noises – little comfort noises – at the back of my throat, as does he. When we cuddle in bed at night, he says, 'I love you so much!' or 'You're such a lovely little person!' There are pet names, too. I'm 'little smelly puss' before a bath, and 'little cleany puss' in my towel on the landing after one; in my dungarees I'm 'you little Herbert!' and when I first wake up and breathe on him I'm his 'little compost heap' or 'little cabbage'. Edwyn kisses me repeatingly, and with great emphasis, in the morning.

There have been other names, of course.

'Just so you know,' he told me last year, 'I have no plans to spend my life with a shrew. Just so you know that. A fishwife shrew with a face like a fucking arsehole that's had...green *acid* shoved up it.'

'You can always just *get out* if you find me so contemptible,' he went on, feet apart, fists clenched, glaring at me over on the settee. 'You have to get behind the *project*, Neve, or get out.'

'What?'

'Get...behind...the project...or...get out!'

'What's "the project"?'

'The *project* is not winding me *up*. The *project* is not trying to get in my head and make me feel like *shit* all the time!'

He shouted this on his way to the bedroom. Twenty minutes later – hot-cheeked, I watched the time on the cooker clock – he came back.

'I don't suppose it would occur to you that I'm miserable...' he said, glumly but scornfully.

'But of *course*,' he went on, 'I *accept*, you've got a much more informed world view than I have! You've got a much deeper world view from collecting people's *glasses*. You've got a much wider knowledge of the world, from being on the *dole*, in the *North*, of *course*!'

There was a lot of shouting from him, back then. Long nights when his agitation, his flinches and side glances, would coalesce into a stronger force. Might you say we were coming to an accommodation, two people who'd always expected, planned, to live their lives alone? I'd never lived with anyone before, I had no idea what it might bring out in me. Certainly I remember feeling that it was his dream world, his symbol world, that we were dragged into during those first arguments, and it frightened me, being given – as I saw it – the part of a training dummy, outfitted in colours, slogans, that I could not see.

Edwyn's tall, over six feet, and these rooms do sometimes look too small for him. When we were rowing, especially, he'd often hunch himself up, round his shoulders, lower his head. Pacing, then pausing, as if in a spotlight, he'd soliloquize, restating his credo, which was – is – *It's freedom that counts*. He'd go on to wonder, haltingly, amazedly, at how he'd boxed himself in (ending up with me in his life, he meant), and when he did address me, it was abstractly, with strange conjectures, ruminations, about what I thought, who I was. 'I know you hate anyone who didn't grow up on benefits,' he'd say, and if I objected he took no notice, or didn't notice, he only continued, talking over me with mounting scorn: 'I know you loathe anyone who didn't grow up in *filth*, on benefits.'

I used to leave my body, in a way, while this went on. It was so incessant, his phrases so concatenated: there was no way in. These were thick, curtain walls.

Edwyn has said since that he feels it's me trying to annihilate him. Strange business, isn't it?

The difference between us, which I did try to keep in mind, was that he really did feel himself under threat back then. He'd had serious heart trouble. An operation. He'd had to lose a lot of weight, stop smoking. Things had settled down by the time we met, but he told me he couldn't feel safe. Not ever again. He was also starting to suffer terribly with his joints. Fibromyalgia, as we later found out. 'I'm paying for something,' he'd snarl, cornered. Or sometimes he'd just sit and sob, and look up at me with frightened eyes when I sat next to him.

Edwyn grew up near Isleworth, an only child. He showed me the house once, the green he used to play on. We walk up that way most Saturdays, unless it's raining: taking the river path, crossing over at Putney. We hold hands, stop to feed the cruising ducks and coots, admire the doughtier dogs we see. I like hearing about Edwyn when he was small. He was a worried little boy, he tells me, when he was three, and four, scared to leave his mother. But then he did use to race to wave at the trains that passed his garden. 'I was rushing towards life!' he says. Later, there was the Nature Club he founded at school, to which he would admit helpers, but no other members. Well, how could he trust them? One early romantic error stays with me, too: how he gave half an Easter egg each to the two girls in his class who liked him, terrified of alienating either one by preferring the other. 'No, they didn't think much of that,' he told me, earnestly, eagerly. 'I went from two girls to no girls!'

My parents' old flat was in Chiswick. I've looked it up: nudging the touchpad to yaw around Spencer Road, to light on Gunyah Court, which proved to be a small block, set between two more robust-looking, bisque-coloured villas. I could picture the living room, having seen a photograph, but nothing else came back.

Sundays have always been for work. I take the settee. Edwyn brings his papers down from his study. With the last of a glass of wine, and always a bunched-up tissue or two (in his office they call him the 'Kleenex Kid', he says), he sits bracketed to the dining table. Also before him is the church candle we light while we eat, and the tin the matchbox is kept in, labelled ALLUMETTES. Sometimes the curled fingers of his right hand lift – like piano hammers, I suppose.

2

Years ago.

I remember: the sky's cold threat. Dishrag clouds, leaking light. And passing Garston: ramifying terraces. Wet slates. Smashed flags.

Lime Street was still under construction: plastic sheets patched the roof, and dripped; the concourse was diminished. My mother stood when she saw me, collected her bags. I stooped to kiss her cold, downy cheek and at that she bared her teeth, lifted her chin.

On the corner of Renshaw Street, the CASHINO was new. In its foil-ribbon window sat a white china tiger, gold-striped, long-necked, and with a clean-toilet gleam. Otherwise, here were the same immemorial chip shops, the sooty junk shops, with their racks of Crimplene costumes, mangy stoles. It was six months since my last visit. Back then my mother had linked arms with me on this stretch; she'd gripped my sleeve and leant in. I hadn't brushed her off, exactly, but it hadn't taken, and she didn't try it now. This was mid-December, a weekday afternoon. We walked quickly, pushing against the sniping wind. Or at least, I thought I was walking at her pace.

'Slow down! Slow down, Neve! Don't zoom off. I'm a pensioner now. I can't *sprint* everywhere!'

With a sort of proud helplessness, she stopped and stood her ground; stoutly in her winter coat, which was ankle-length, grey-green, padded in rings. Her being 'a pensioner', 'an old *lady*, now' was a favoured new plea, back then. When she first retired, she said she felt lost. She said so often, if coyly. No one was interested, of course, and hence this new tack. Now she was kitted out. She had her Saga subscription, she told me, and she was vivacious on the subject of her new shopping trolley: 'No, Neve, it's brilliant, for a *pensioner*!'

'Shall I take some of those bags?' I said. 'What's in them?'

'Oh. Just, different things. Things you might be interested in. Since you *refuse* to come to the house, I have to bring everything out with me, don't I?'

We were going to the cinema. There was a café on Bold Street where she wanted to get a drink first, she said, a new tea room, but as we turned the corner, she stopped again.

'*Oh* ... shit,' she said, and then she stepped back into a doorway.

'What is it?'

'Tss ... Someone I don't want to see. Old boyfriend.'

She pressed her shoulder against the shutter, turned further away.

'Really? When from?'

'A few years ago. Before Rodger.'

'Is he going to walk past?'

'No. I think he was going in a shop, but – wait a second. Just wait, Neve. Just wait, please…OK, yes, come on, let's go quickly. Come on, and try and look engrossed in conversation. Look animated, Neve!'

She took my arm now, as we steamed away, so here was her face again, crowned with her red fleece cloche, banded by her purple-framed glasses, smiling purposefully up at me.

'This is nice,' I said, as we slid along the blond wood benches. I wiped a port in the fogged-up window, while she arranged her bags next to her, then her hat, her scarf, her too-big thermal gloves.

'Yes. I've been in here before. I don't usually like going in places on my own, places I don't know, but I'd been past a few times and it seems nice, doesn't it? Friendly.'

We ordered a pot of green tea each, and then both stood up again to take off our coats.

'So what boyfriend was that?'

'Oh. *Well* – it was after I moved to Catharine Street, do you remember I went out with that Jewish man, Simon, for a while, with the ponytail. No? Well, I *did*. But after *him* I started seeing that man, Greg, and, yes, we went out a few times, oh, but I could never ring him, you know, because he was *so* busy, I had to wait for him to ring *me*, or – big trouble. Big troub. Anyway – I didn't even like him very much. He repaired sash windows and he was quite open with me that he ripped people off. No shame about that. I've warned quite a few people since then, who've mentioned they're having their windows done. I say, Well, *whatever you do*, don't get

Greg Martin to do it, he'll rip you off. Anyway, so he *did* ring me one afternoon and he dumped me, you see, and then even though I hadn't been out with him that often and I didn't like him very much, I sort of – yes, I did get very upset about that, and ended up writing him this letter, which I regret now, so…'

'Oh dear.'

'Mm…Yes. And – no, he's not a very nice man, as it turned out, so…'

Her hair was chin-length then: thick, grey, limp. Behind her glasses her wide-set eyes looked frightened. She even looked frightened when the waitress set down our teapots, which were transparent and had a plunger.

'How do we get the tea out?' she whispered, as the girl moved off. 'Oh, no! Come back!'

'I thought you'd been here before.'

'Oh, yes, well, I couldn't work it then either!'

Back in the summer she'd had a birthday M&S voucher she said she wouldn't use: did I want it? I did. She'd started her turn then as we crossed the floor to Hosiery: surrounded, as we were, by strange statuary. My mother blenched extravagantly at the gussied-up torsos, blinking hard like someone had flashed a torch in her eyes, saying she *couldn't* understand why *anyone* would buy, wear, matching underwear.

'Yes, it's *such* a relief I never, *ever* have to do *any* of that again,' she said. 'Yuck yuck *yuck*. Just – no. I can't even bear it in films now.

I have to close my eyes!'

My mother went to the pictures a lot, back then, always to FACT, Liverpool's new cinema-gallery-café. I was often surprised by what she saw. I think she saw whatever they put on. As to what she thought of these films: hard to say. Her opinions were offered so cautiously. She might say something had been 'Too long,' or 'So violent!' I always felt terrible when she said, of something she'd looked forward to, and with only just a shade less brightness to her voice, that it had been 'Not what I expected.' That even became a sort of sad catchphrase between Edwyn and me for a while, which I felt guilty about, slightly queasy about, sometimes. Once he asked me, 'Does everything your mother tries end in disaster?' Which made me feel desperate! But those were the stories she told me, so that's what I'd pass on. I didn't overdo that (I hope), but sometimes we swapped confidences. Once, when I first came to stay, when we were lying in bed. I don't know what prompted that discussion, of his mother on the loo.

'I used to hear these dreadful noises in the morning,' Edwyn said. And pleating his lips, and narrowing his eyes, to more precisely recall, so that his eyebrow quills stood rampant, he said, 'Gurgling and spluttering. Like bad plumbing. Which it was, I suppose. Her grossly over-functioning digestion! The thundering waterfall of her first piss! Terrifying. I thought bodies were terrifying. But then –' wistfully – 'puberty did its work – soon I couldn't wait to get up there!'

I told him:

'I have memories of my mum on the toilet, too. Noises in the night. She had IBS. Stress-induced. I heard her crying once and got up and found her sitting with her nightie all gathered up between her knees. She said, "Leave me, please, go back to bed, Neve! Just leave me!" And there were these little splutters. In the morning I wondered if I'd dreamt it.'

'Oh dear. Poor old thing. "Just leave me."'

'Mmm…Well, she wasn't old then. She was my age. No. A bit older…'

I'd thought about that night when she got married again, too. She had a nasty hangover on her wedding day. When I got to her flat that morning she was quailing in a corner of the settee, and retching, and sobbing, a bucket with some Dettol in it at her feet.

In FACT my mother queued for our tickets, smiled as she showed her membership card. In the cinema she moved along the row. Reaching the middle, she stopped and put all of her bags down on the seat to her left, between us, and then she started un-popping the poppers on her coat.

'What are you doing?'

'What?'

'Where am I going to sit?'

'Oh. No. I can't sit next to people.'

'Hey? We've come together. We always sit together…'

Here she showed her teeth again, looked cornered, angry.

'No. *No.* I always go on my own!'

•

How did it come to that?

Remember. Soon after they were married. That dusty old pub. I was in town to see Kerrigan, but she'd been badgering me to give her her old keys back, and I kept forgetting to post them. She was going to meet Rodger and his friends for a drink, she said, in the Crown. His 'artist friends', she called them, and they proved easy to spot: a raucous group of men, in paint-scabbed fishermen's jumpers. My mother wasn't quite sitting with them, though, but on a low stool a few feet behind Rodger. She wore a familiar expression: too eager, half-sly, while no one spoke to her, or looked at her. She held her empty half-pint glass up by her chin, and grinned hopelessly. Kerrigan was waiting outside, I told her I couldn't stop, but still, bravely, and to little effect, when I crouched down next to her, she said, '*Everyone*, this is my *daughter*.'

It must be a dreadful cross: this hot desire to join in with people who don't want you. This need to burrow in. But, then – perhaps I'm not one to talk. A few years later, I was buying tickets for a preview of Terence Davies' new film: in Liverpool, so I asked if she wanted to come. 'Oh, *yes*,' she said. 'And am I *allowed* to bring Rodger?'

Of Time and the City ends with fireworks dashing skywards, pop-pop-pop, raining blue sparks over the Pier Head. The voiceover says:

Good night, ladies; good night, sweet ladies; good night,
good night, good night...

Following the producers up onto the stage, Davies took his bow and I clapped hard. I was deeply moved by his flushed face, his clasped hands. Here was an artist to the tips of his fingers, and he'd been treated so shabbily, so disgracefully. He'd said somewhere, 'I lost all hope.' Wouldn't you call that sickening?

Later, as we were standing to leave, as I was getting my bag from under the seat, my mother said,

'Oh, well, it's all very well for him going on about Liverpool, but he doesn't live here any more, does he! And what's with that Donald Sinden voice?'

She was looking to Rodger.

'Don't be squalid, Mum. That was a beautiful work of art.'

She pulled a face now. An indignant face: mouth gaping. She put a hand to her chest.

'Squalid, *moi*?'

Rodger yawned, in his horse-ish way. Again, he didn't look at her, but pronounced, finally, as he zipped his coat,

'Not art. Fart.'

Rodger was a painter. He'd taught for years at the College of Art. Elsewhere I'd asked my mother what she thought of his work, which hung throughout his house.

'Oh, well, I'm not *allowed* an opinion, you see, not having been to *art school*,' she said. 'My opinion's worthless, apparently, so...but I think they're all crap, yes. Absolute *crap*, so...'

'Have you told him that?'

'Oh, he doesn't listen to what I say!'

•

16

Edwyn and I got married this year. Against both of our instincts, I think, but undertaken on his solicitor's advice, all part of putting his affairs in order. Everyone named in his previous will being dead, as he put it, and he wanted to take care of me. 'Do something useful,' he said. We went to the register office in Chelsea. A small, sunny room. An old wooden desk. There were no guests, just the two witnesses. Afterwards, outside, Edwyn had one of them take some photos on her phone. It was the hottest, driest day. Blazing sun. Nonetheless Edwyn had brought his umbrella out with him, so in each shot he's holding that, or leaning on it. In the last snap he's using it to point the way: a thin black signal, down to the river for a drink.

3

That was in June. We didn't go away. We were due to drive down to Devon, but Edwyn's condition flared up, and he couldn't face the journey. Instead he stayed in bed for three days, then went back to work, desperately unhappy, difficult to soothe.

Those were a tough few weeks. Every day dawned humid, sticky. No cooling gusts on Cromwell Gardens. The thunder only proclaimed itself. I used to sit here with the windows open, the blinds down. Just me and the flies: quick-quick-slow, in the well of the room.

I had nowhere to be. In term time I'd be teaching on Wednesdays and Thursdays. (I didn't miss that.) And then on Friday afternoons I used to see a psychotherapist. Miss Moore – Amy – was based in Gospel Oak, in the Ford Road 'Serenity Centre', an old Deaf School, I believe, now a warren of treatment rooms; long corridors lined with crowded noticeboards and empty coat pegs. I saw her for seven months, but gave my notice a few days before the wedding, finally overwhelmed by the powerfully childish sense of drag which had started to get into me, almost as soon as I sat down with her; before I sat down, when I set off from home.

I felt good as I left the last session, at least; delivered into my old silence, walking down the hill. I was glad to get the time back. Not incidentally, I was glad to save the money. I thought about the things I could do with it, as I waited for the tube, and then as I stood at the end of the carriage, swaying in the hot, rushing air.

Edwyn got in that night, as usual, at about half past eight. He called out, 'Phew, bloody hell!' as he climbed the stairs, and looked nice when he appeared on our landing, with his sunglasses dangling and his hair damp; his blue linen shirt untucked, but sticking to his round stomach and his back.

'Hello!' I said.

'What's all this?'

'It's detritus. I'm sorting things out.'

I stood up and took the wastepaper basket into the kitchen. Edwyn still had his rucksack on. He stood with his mouth slightly open, recovering from his walk.

'You're not going to leave that there, are you?'

'No, I'm just emptying this.'

'Do you have to have the blinds down?'

'I do. But you can open them now.'

I stood at the sink, washing the dust from my nails. Soon enough

Edwyn was behind me, looking at what I'd made for tea, giving it a creaturely sniff.

'Are you OK?' I said. 'Let's have a cuddle now.'

'Hm…Yes, I'm OK. I think I will have to avoid the Central line till the weather breaks, though.'

'Oh dear. Yes, go a different way. Poor thing. Prr prr. You smell nice.'

'Don't I smell horrible and sweaty?'

'No, I like it. Prr prr. Lovely Mr Pusskins.'

'Lovely *Mrs* Pusskins! Prr prr.'

4

It's seven years now, since I packed those boxes, moving out of my place in Tempus Tower and into my friend Margaret's spare room. I was there for two years, in the end, then in Glasgow for three years, on my own again. I knew a few people in London when I moved down, but I haven't sought them out much (nor they me, as it goes). I have made some new friends. I find I like how things work down here, seeing people once a month, if that. Once every six months. I'm very happy to spend my time with Edwyn. I love our evenings, our routines.

Still, there is an occasional surprise. This January I got a text from Bridie, my best friend, as was. Doggedly, affrontedly, long after we were sick of each other, that's what we called each other. She left Manchester about five years ago, to teach drama abroad, and it was only then that this stubborn alliance could dissolve. She wrote to me sometimes, about the troupe she'd joined, but less frequently as the months went by. Her updates were entertaining, as these things

go. Long, dashing, offhand bursts. In her new gang, there was someone who'd been in *EastEnders*, she told me, a hard man run to fat,
who she'd been sleeping with. Her boss, too, she started sleeping
with. What did he sound like? A freewheeling type, a patched-up,
pot-bellied minstrel, who wore novelty socks, drank a lot, again,
and 'Stank like shit!' as she put it. She was in Russia the last time she
wrote, doing *The Wind in the Willows* for schoolchildren. Her new
best friend was called Olesya, she said. They'd recently got drunk
with a cosmonaut, she said. I wrote half of a reply to that before
deciding I couldn't match her brio.

I don't know if she knew I'd moved to Scotland, but word had
reached her, evidently, about my being down here. She'd been home
for Christmas, she wrote, and was going to be in London before
flying to Moscow. Did I want to meet? She needed to buy some
boots, so I suggested the Nero near Westfield.

I saw her first, just ahead of me in the queue. That was her
little head, her little topknot, crowning a busy hive of flossy blonde
hair. She wore a cone-shaped, carrot-coloured coat, grey tights, blue
Converse.

'Bridie.'

'Oh, my God! Hi!'

'Hiya. Shall I get that table?'

'Yes! Quick! What would you like?'

'Oh. Soy cappuccino, please. Small one. Thanks.'

I got us the window seat, then moved her bags: a backpack and
a long, sausage-y holdall.

24

Bridie had been working in Venice, she'd said, in her text. But as it turned out, when I asked her what that was like, she hadn't quite made it there.

'Oh, I wasn't really in *Venice*.'

'Were you not?'

'Oh, no. I could have *got* to Venice if I'd wanted to take three buses and have no way to get back! I was living on an industrial estate! I don't know where it was!'

'Do you just get trafficked around, then?'

'Yeah! You just answer adverts. So I was on this, yeah, industrial estate, living in this cupboard! No, it was bigger than a cupboard. There was me and one other teacher, so-called, from Birmingham. Our landlady had no hands, so she'd bring our trays in like this—' Bridie mimed the action. 'There was nothing in town. Total shithole.'

'Hadn't you settled down in Moscow?'

'Pffft. Well, maybe. I mean, I am going back now. I was living with this man called Ivan.'

'That's exciting.'

'I know. He is a bastard, though. He's impregnated two women while I've been gone. He's given another one herpes. I check his emails.'

'Can you read Russian now?'

'Mm...I can read what he writes. Anyway, he kept flying out to see me but I just sent him back. He kept screaming at me. He said there's a special time in a man's life when he has to have two women.

I was his number one, he said. But he did need two, though. Bit depressing, really. All the women he likes are just terrible-looking, too!'

'Go on.'

'In Russia if you say you fell in love at first sight, it translates as "I fell down". This other one he's been with recently is older than him, and he first went with her when he was fifteen or something. Ivan says when he met her he fell down, so he was fucking furious when I found a picture of her. Because she looks like shit. She looks like a granny. Basically he just screams abuse at me. But I am going back to live with him now. He has kept chasing me around the world to ask me, so…If this visa comes through, anyway. I've got to go up there before seven.'

'Up where? The embassy?'

'Yeah. The embassy. I'm down as a "consultant" at this university in the far north of Moscow. But that's not real. I'll find something. Recently I infiltrated this group of politicos. They're all my friends now. I'm this children's entertainer, English teacher-tutor, fuck knows what they think, except that I'm with Ivan. Their last meeting was in this place called the American Grill. They were all sat around a table the size of this room. There was this handsome young man there called Ilya. Someone had bought him a pair of boxer shorts with dollar bills all over them, so he was wearing nothing but them. Basically Russians go out and act disgusting. That's what they do. The women are beautiful but lots of them don't speak. The men smoke cigars. Ilya is seeing this heiress now. She's the daughter of one of Putin's cronies. She's a sort of Paris Hilton figure. He's seeing her to raise his profile…'

Bridie took a long sip of her coffee here, and then she put down her cup and beamed at me, stretching her arms out before her, holding a shudder like a note.

'You are quite teacherish now,' I said.

'What does *that* mean?' she said.

We walked up to the shops, into the throat of the wind. People were moving slowly, obstructively, in both directions: only these little tiptoe scutters when a gust caught them: arms lifted, bags.

'Ivan would be furious if I turned up in these,' Bridie said, holding out one foot as we rode up the escalator. 'I've got to get some serious boots!'

She changed her shoes as soon as we left Westfield, crouched in the doorway of Toni & Guy. She half-posted the huge box into a bin, tied her Converse to her backpack.

'Do you live near here?'

'Yes, not far. Couple of stops. Do you want to come for a cup of tea?'

'Yes, please! I'm nosey!'

Knock knock knock went her boot heels as we hurried up Cromwell Gardens. It was five o'clock. The light was going.

•

She was terribly polite, in the flat. She sat on the sofa with her hands on her knees; looked around wide-eyed, smiling. Edwyn was in, at the table, work laid out in front of him. There was less talk of incident and adventure now. We drank our cups of tea, then I saw Bridie out.

'He's attractive!' she whispered, mouthed, on the stairs.

'You're living my dream!' she said.

Edwyn made no comment, when I went back upstairs, and I felt baffled, frightened, by what my old life had been.

The next night, coming home from work, I surfaced from the tube to an email from my agent. My cousin Patricia had found her online, she wrote. She wanted to speak to me urgently about my father. Should she pass my details on, or not? What would I like her to say? She hoped everything was all right? Out on the street my phone buzzed again. I bit off my glove to listen to the message. The same cousin had written to Edwyn. (How on earth did she know about him?)

It was late. Cold. I dipped my head and met the wet wind, feeling queasy, harried. There seemed to be a party happening at a bar I passed: a gulping beat, pulsing lights. I got as far as the glass doors, thinking I'd just have a drink, but gave up when I saw the press of bodies inside.

Edwyn was insistent that nothing I'd heard meant that my father was dead. I knew that he was dead.

'Well, call this woman and find out,' he said.

'Well, no, because if he isn't, I don't want to get dragged into anything. I'll think about it in the morning.'

A few days later Edwyn got home to find me still crying, my teeth chattering. I couldn't get warm, though the heating was on. Nor could I feel clean, though I'd been sitting in the bath every morning, dousing the coarse gooseflesh. My hands felt grubby, and my face, and my feet. I would keep shuddering, as if I were trying to adjust to the change. I loitered by the kettle. Then long sips, deep breaths. I was treating myself as if I were a nervous imbecile, really.

'What's the matter with you?' Edwyn said.

I was on the settee with my blanket. He was standing in the kitchen doorway.

'I don't understand,' he said. 'You're an intelligent woman. Did you imagine he was going to live for ever?'

'No.'

'We all feel guilt, honey. Guilt is just what you feel when this happens.'

'OK. Fine.'

'He's dead, you're alive, you're guilty, it's desolate,' Edwyn said. 'Sooner or later you are going to have to get over this.'

'OK.'

'That's just realism, honey.'

'Great. Thanks. Can you leave it now, please?'

'I'm happy to leave it.' Here he walked back into the kitchen, started banging the pans about. 'I know I'm just an irritant to you. Everything I say and do and think…When I do speak you want me to *shut up*, and when I don't you wonder why I'm not talking to you. If only I'd kept my father's Luger. I could have just blown my fucking brains out, how's that?'

This is frustrating, about Edwyn. That when I'm upset he panics.

'I don't feel guilty,' I said, or called out.

He came back to the doorway then, and looked at me keenly: a lawyer who'd marked an inconsistency.

'What?' I said.

'You don't feel you were unfair to him?'

'No.'

'Oh, I must have misunderstood you, I'm sorry. Yesterday you said you felt guilty.'

'Did I? Well, I don't now.'

'And you're sitting there snivelling…'

'I am,' I said.

I told him I'd been reading the list my mother made of the things my father had done to her. A strange document I'd taken years ago. I had thought it might check my tears.

'Listen to this,' I said. *'Slapped, strangled, thumbs twisted. Hit about head while breast-feeding. Hit about head while suffering migraine. Several kicks at base of spine. Hot pan thrown, children screaming.'*

'Oh, she kept a list, did she?' Edwyn said.

'Not at the time. She had to write it down for her solicitor. Not that anyone listened.'

'I see. And how long were they married?'

'Eight years.'

'And she could remember that far back, could she? Did she keep a diary?'

'Did she keep a diary? What a weird, horrible question.'

He frowned slightly, but he was smiling too, his eyes were glittering.

'It was a genuine question,' he said. And as he went on, he spoke slowly, softly, as if I were very stupid. Stupid and volatile.

'She must have a very good memory, that's all. Some people do. Of course they do. That's all I wanted to know. I'm interested. It's *very* interesting to me. That she'd remember, quite so clearly, all of these…what might you call them?'

'Assaults,' I said.

He tilted his head, musing on whether to allow that.

'Well – incidents,' he said.

I had another sleepless night, that night, Edwyn snuffling next to me, and outside, for a while, our little fox yelping. Incredulous little yelps.

5

The funeral was at Springfield Crematorium in Garston, very close to my father's house. Most of his family live around there, or in Aigburth, or Speke. He was the oldest of fourteen, and the first to die, too. 'It's put the wind up everyone, you can imagine!' my aunt Christine told me.

I hadn't seen any of my aunts or my uncles or my cousins in fifteen years. Not since our Saturday 'access' visits.

I nodded at my brother, at the gates. I hadn't seen him since I'd left home either. He'd grown tubby, gone grey. There were whole patches of white in his short, schoolboy haircut. Standing by the wall, he seemed uncomfortable, suspicious even, half-leering, half-wincing when people went over to say hello. The woman he was with shared his look. She held his arm and glowered.

The past was before us. The Mulqueens gathered and here were faces, characters from long ago.

Leaning forward on the lectern, confidentially, our uncle Peter gave the eulogy:

'Now, Barry lived life to the full. He was the first of the O'Donnell grandkids, and he was *spoiled rotten*. And he continued to spoil him*self* rotten, I think it's fair to say.'

I'd been to the house. I made a dash for it, four days after I heard the news. Christine met me at Lime Street.

I said some strange things to her, seeing those rooms again. I wept, and sobbed. I clenched my fists in terror. Poor woman. And what a nice woman. She always was nice to us.

'It's like he's just stepped out, isn't it?' she said. 'When I came back I noticed there was a cup of tea made, by the kettle...'

I nodded.

Christine had found him. She'd been coming once a week, she told me, cleaning from the ground floor up. He was on the second flight of stairs.

The house felt very lonely. Like a lonely child's lair, really. The brave business of self-solace everywhere in evidence (to my eyes, anyway). His comforts. His acquisitions. Stores of treats. Discarded novelties.

The little kitchen was crowded with equipment, but all of it dusty, greasy. Here was a rice cooker. A meat slicer. A SodaStream. And so much food. Family-sized tubs of sweets, stacked up. Italian biscuits in cellophane sacks tied with thin gold cord. There were bags and bags of fancy pasta, half a dozen tins of *confit de canard*. I opened the fridge.

'Jesus.'

'Oh, yes, your dad was a demon for cheese!'

'It looks like a cheese counter.'

'I know, I know. Barry was not going to be told what he couldn't have. No way. Look at this: goose fat. Mayonnaise. Custard...'

The living room had changed. A huge red sofa filled half of the space now.

'This was his centre of operations, really,' Christine said. 'Once he had his iPad. That was his window on the world. He was ordering food from the four corners of the globe then.'

'He got much bigger.'

'He did. To be honest, Neve, I don't know that you would have recognized him, at the end.'

After the reception, my uncle Patrick drove us back to the station, with poor Edwyn folded in the back, knees by his chin, watching Liverpool go by, the spread of estates near town.

'There must have been a lot of bombs, I suppose, around here,' he said.

It was a wet evening, the air tinted purple. Rain trembled across the window. At my feet I had a Bag for Life, containing the iPad, and the few papers that had turned up. (My father had burnt most of them, Patrick thought.) There was no will.

'God, he'd be sick, you know, to think you had all that power!' Patrick said. 'All that info!'

•

It was ten days, from that first phone call to seeing his boat-sized coffin slide away. The mind scrambles. At one point I cried to Edwyn that my father had been 'the sensitive one'! (Not untrue, from a certain angle.) The tears would keep coming: pity, dread, succeeding each other relentlessly. Extraordinary, really. When had I last had a tender feeling towards my father? I think I was six. He turned forty when I was six, and I remember getting terribly upset then, worried for him, because he was 'old'. He would have scoffed at that, I'm sure. My mother did. Once, I tried to kiss him, again when I was about that age, only he wiped it off, pulled a face at my brother. A gratified face, a sort of 'get her' face. After that – nothing. Extreme inhibition, that was all. Ceding slowly to a dull sense of waiting it out. And that contempt, perhaps, that Edwyn has noted (and he isn't wrong); I suppose that must have started to make itself at home in me then, during those weekends. How horrible. What a legacy. Something in me balked, thinking of that, but it was no good, I felt that rank and creaky old outrage, getting to its feet again at the back of the room, ready to pour out whatever was still pooling in its cup.

It was his whetted look, I found, that I remembered most vividly. His stout expectation. How had that endured: life, knocks? But it had. He was 'Just a big kid, really,' Christine said. Well, quite. Somehow he was. A greedy child. A tyrant child. And for fifteen years, every Saturday, my brother and I were laid on to service him. To listen to him. To be frightened by him, should he feel like it. As a child with his toys, he exercised a capricious rule, and as with any little imperator, his rage was hellish were his schemes not reverenced. One wrong word unlatched a sort of chaos. The look in his eyes then! Licensed hatred. The keenest hunger. As the plates were swept off the counter, kicked around the floor. As the sofa was upended, pictures torn from the walls. He had to triumph. And how he'd triumph, having no resource but his shamelessness.

'Thought you'd got one over on me, didn't you!' Digging his fingers in, showing his top teeth. 'Didn't you, hey?'

His hair was black then, just threaded with white. After a rage it hung in pieces over his dark, panting face.

Not that he confined himself to us. There were all sorts of satisfactions to be had, for the restless bully about town. My father used to lay into shop assistants. People behind the counters in fast-food restaurants. I think he went to those places to shout: that low guile among his many atavisms, for here were young people without authority or status. He jutted his head forward, his face darkened, and he poured forth a scalding fury. (His chips weren't crispy enough!) Peremptory enquiries were repeated with a jab of his finger. The answers were as dirt. ('You want to find whoever told you that, and kick them, hard.') Insults came last, about weight or brain power. And then we'd have to leave with him. All eyes on us in a space gone quiet.

So he proceeded, unchecked, more or less. (Runaway wife aside.) His antics surely dismayed people: his family, wouldn't you think? But what could you do? He was aggressive, not bright, none of which makes for a person you want to engage with if you can help it. Instead – I did it myself when I was older – you smiled, tried to meet him halfway, just as you might encourage a baby, and give all your warm attention to a baby, to get it to behave. He was like a baby. There was that appalling, babyish, naming-triumph to his pronouncements. He liked to point, and he liked to bark what he saw. Out and about, sampling life, he'd shout zealously: 'Big bum!' 'Bleach blonde!' 'Pop socks!'

'What about pop socks?' I'd say, my voice level, friendly, curious.

At which he'd beam and chomp the air a little, snorting like a bull, and then he'd point again, with his fat freckled hand, at some poor woman doing her shopping:

'Pop socks!'

'Big bum!'

He had a waddling walk, being toddler-shaped: short legs, his stomach a full sail. Walking ahead, he'd lift his leg to fart and then turn to look at us with dog-like surprise. This was our father in a carnival spirit, but I do hope I'm giving credit to his range…When the mood took him, he was also a great explainer of the world. A bold scheme for someone as thick as him but, with a chuckling authority, he would confide his considered assessments to, let's say, the eight- and ten-year-old children in the back of his car:

'Women like your mother. They are a particular *breed*. You will find that. You will notice that.'

'Your grandmother really is filthy. That house of hers. She's very *sluttish*. Just look at her cuffs sometime, or the collars of her shirts or her jerseys. They are black with grease. We all noticed it. Thatcher-ites like her are really creepy people. You'll find that. They don't *know* how to keep themselves clean.'

My brother stopped going to see him when he was fifteen, after my father punched him in the face. I had to keep at it. 'Just one more year,' as my mother said, 'just keep the peace, please.' And I was the one he wanted, that became clear. There were no threats when my brother didn't show up, no triumphant withdrawals of maintenance or accusations of sexual abuse. (He'd fingered my grandfather and a teacher at different times, when I tried to get my weekends back. He wrote lurid letters to my mother, with a swash-buckling tone, and speechified to his brothers and sisters, in their kitchens every Saturday, or so my brother said.)

Still, things did go badly for him that last year, when I was show-ing up alone. He lost his job, lost his driving licence, for good this time. He wasn't shopping at M&S any more. I was peacefully in-curious about all of this. I said nothing. When he brought it up, in his wounded, blustery way, I didn't respond. His friend Frank had brought him some food, he said.

'Frank's a Christian, you know. He called it a tithe. I said I'll accept it in the spirit of wealth redistribution!'

Frank was a large Chinese man who used to work with my father at AB Foods. I hadn't met him, only heard about him. They often went for 'banquets' together at the Yang Sing. Later Frank worked in the council office with my mother. She was unaware of the connection, at first. One Saturday, she saw Frank in town and said hello. Cunningly, Frank said, 'Er…Who are you again?'

'Apparently she greeted him like he was a long-lost relative!' my father told me. 'It was very odd. Frank says they all think she's weird, at work. Yes, there's something very off there. Very creepy.'

There was only one other friend that I ever caught sight of. Con appeared during that last year, came over twice for lunch, then wasn't mentioned again. He was an ex-colleague of my father's too, and younger than him, as Frank had been. He was short, slight, sceptical-looking. He was in the early stages of multiple sclerosis, my father revealed, announced, while Con was out of earshot. I don't know if he ever met Con's wife, but he liked to make remarks about her. Winking at me and mugging, 'She who must be obeyed!' Con was sometimes receptive to these remarks, sometimes not. The notion of a wife was perhaps by then quite fantastical to my father. (I remember my friend Paul Powell telling me how, aged nine or ten, imagining the future with his best friend, they would discuss – place great emphasis on – 'taking camping trips with our *wives*'.)

On Con's second visit, my father came down from the bathroom and said, 'I think you need to go and clean up, up there.'

Con looked up, but it was me he was talking to.

'Clean up?'

Here my father performed a familiar trick: judging my question stupid, he didn't answer, he just sat down, put his feet up, locked his gaze on the TV.

'What do you mean?' I said.

'You'll see what I mean.'

I went upstairs. The bathroom looked clean. The toilet looked clean. (The cistern was still filling up after his flush.) I lifted the seat and saw two drops of dried blood, both tiny, barely more than pinheads. I took a piece of toilet paper and spat on it, rubbed the drops away.

'I couldn't see anything,' I said, coming back into the living room.

'Look again!' he said, not looking up.

I went back upstairs, stood on the landing for a few moments then came down again, sat down again.

'All gone?'

At first I didn't answer.

'All gone?'

'Yes, it's all gone,' I said, looking at the TV.

A few moments later, my father piped up again.

'Women just aren't naturally clean, are they?' he said, turning to Con.

But still the weeks ticked down. On my last Saturday with him my father had looked out a photograph of himself.

'One of the few pictures of me in existence, that!' he said, nodding at it. 'You can have that, if you want, take it with you!'

In grey photo-fog: a small fat child. Thick spectacles. A sad glint of mischief in his smile.

'Why don't you like having your photo taken?'

'Oh. Don't know. Never have. Yes, your nana felt very guilty about that picture. I got so upset!'

I didn't take it with me. I looked at it from where I stood. Didn't pick it up.

That should have been it. My time served. It was quite easy to forget he existed, I found. To leave those rooms to gentle decay. But at the end of my first semester – I was at Manchester University – my mother forwarded a letter to halls. His handwriting. No note. Just a ticket to a concert at the Philharmonic, in a week's time. Even had I felt inclined to, I couldn't have gone. I wrote to say so: 'I'm afraid I have exams that week. I hope you have a good night.' Soon enough, again without a note, another ticket, for a concert a few weeks later.

Well, I went. Encouraged by my mother again, the mad old pimp. After the concert we walked over to the Kebab House on Hardman Street, a place he used to take my brother and me after similar evenings at the Phil., which were always a trial: feeling so shut down inside, even to music.

My father made my brother sick in the Kebab House, once: that was a memory. He was sick at the table. It poured out onto his plate with a hot little burp. This was just after I'd turned vegetarian. My father had had to lump that, but my brother following suit?

'No!' he'd barked. 'Lamb! He's having lamb!'

And nor did he leave it there. As my poor brother chewed his first mouthful, my father glared at him hungrily, excitedly.

'I was right, wasn't I?' he said. 'You wanted lamb! Wasn't I right?'

He kept asking, until my brother nodded. Not enough. My

brother had to say, 'Yes.' My father watched every mouthful he ate of that meal, with a look on his face that was truly obscene.

He was in his pomp again tonight. Employed again, apparently.

'And like I say, don't worry about *cost*, at all,' he said, 'order what you like, because…'

Here, grimacing, he half-stood to pull his wallet from the back pocket of his jeans. Then he held his wallet up, and in a tick-tick of unsticking plastic, four sheathed credit cards unfolded and hung there. He went from top to bottom.

'Credit limit: five K. Credit limit: two K. Five hundred pounds on this one. This one has gone up to two thousand. I don't ask for it, they just write and tell you it's increased!'

He ordered lamb. I had two of the vegetable side dishes. Looking after the waiter as he left, then turning to look at the owner at the back, and to take in the other diners, my father said, 'They all think you're my fancy piece! My secretary!' (Pronounced 'secutary'.)

He asked about my course next, but pulled a face when I told him.

'Sounds like posing to me!' He turned again to the waiters, the owner.

'Does it? That's a shame. I'm not posing.'

'You're going to alienate a lot of people with all this posing!' he said.

'Ah, well…'

From his jacket's inside pocket, he pulled out a programme for the coming season at the Phil. He'd marked the concerts we were going to see together. Every fortnight.

'Oh. I work on Saturdays, I'm afraid,' I said. 'You haven't bought tickets, have you?'

He didn't answer that. Instead came that wounded huff-puff, harrumph. His eyes narrowed. Just then, our food arrived; his huge grey hump of meat, his chunky chips, so that distracted him, he set to it. We ate in silence for a while, and in my mind, then, I left the scene: out into the bracing cold, down the hill to Lime Street. I could call Bridie from the train, go out when I got back.

'Where's your brother living these days?'

'Still at home. He's only seventeen.'

My father frowned, lifted his chin. His expression was one of supreme indifference.

'He wants to do History at Leeds, I think. Last I heard, that's what Mum said.'

'Hmph...'

'What's that?'

'Because we were all quite concerned about him, you know. The *organizations* he was joining.'

'Organizations?'

'He's a follower, Neve. He's always been a follower.'

'What organizations are you talking about?'

He chewed a bit of his dead animal, swallowed. Then he took another mouthful. Was he going to answer me?

'Dad?' I said. He took his time, then wiped his mouth with the napkin he'd tucked in to his collar.

'Oh, just a nasty group of people. Group of friends. We all

44

noticed it. I mean, real NF stuff.'

'NF stuff? Last I heard he was going to SWP meetings. What are you talking about?'

The look he gave me then was a threatening look. A thuggish look. I felt the familiar quickening, inside: something being slit open, gone through. But I continued.

'I mean, *is* there still an NF?' I said, smiling, interested. 'Perhaps you don't know, but his girlfriend's Pakistani. Sara? They've been together two years now. They want to go to Leeds together. But that aside, I'm not sure where you've got the NF from.'

'Oh – well. Is she?' he said, and he pushed out his lips, looked over my shoulder. 'Hm…Well…that's encouraging.'

I didn't order any dessert. He got ice cream. Three scoops. I watched him tuck into the chocolate-flavoured scoop. Trying to be conciliatory, I said,

'That ice cream looks vegan to me. That's thoughtful of them.'

I picked up my coffee spoon and smiled. I thought he'd like that. To share something. To conspire. I was wrong. His expression then was of alarm, and then of hatred. That I'd take his ice cream from him.

'Oh. Sorry,' I said.

He scowled, looked down, took another soft spoonful.

A month passed, then another ticket arrived: rattling in its envelope, again, merrily forwarded by my mother, again. ('The NF?' she'd said. 'How *strange*.') I returned it with a letter saying I didn't want to stay in touch. 'I'm not interested,' I wrote. 'This isn't working and I want to get on with my life.' Stupid letter. Wrong-headed. How did my father read it? As a challenge, of course. A 'spicing up', even. What followed was a struggle. There was nowhere he wasn't, suddenly, and his efforts only drew strength from each refusal. It was like trying to deny an excited octopus. Repeated unhookings. It took a sort of disappearing act on my part, in the end, to get away. After which, he started sending my brother tickets. (My mother told me.) But six months in, with no reply, those letters stopped.

Anyway. All of this came back to me, then subsided. The fascination with old things rediscovered (like opening those boxes) soon wears off. Christine told me that when her father died (that's my grandfather) she ran all the way from the hospital back to their house. Miles and miles, in the winter, and without a coat.

6

Can the future be a white expanse? Can you run in, heart pounding?

I find I've never given much thought to the future. Beyond that sense of getting away. Derelictions, you see, left and right. Yet here I am.

Edwyn and I had to face each other when we got married, and hold both hands. After the registrar, we repeated, 'I promise to love you and care for you for as long as we both shall live.' Potent words. It felt incredible to say them, to hear them.

His hands ache now, all day, but especially in the morning. I used to rub them with oil first thing: a carrier oil and a 'relaxing' oil, mixed up by my finger in a medicine cup. 'It *smells* nice,' he'd say, his poor staunch mitts on the towel I put over the duvet. But it didn't help, not really. His condition is a scold, I'm learning. Edwyn's wary of door handles, these days. A tight tap. A heavy kettle. He gets put down so spitefully, should he forget himself. A DIY jag – 'Got to keep things shipshape!' he says – will leave him moaning, his wrists swollen; he rides his bike and a hip joint burns, so for days he can't settle, can't walk, can only hobble and hiss.

'It feels like someone's going at me with a *welding torch*,' he says, giving me a meaningful look.

Sleep is difficult, too. Whisky helps him drop off. Which is fine, until he starts snoring. In the past I might have tried to roll him over, or given him a nudge, but that doesn't seem fair any more. Instead I tend to get up, lie on the settee, roam the flat. Recently, abroad in the bathroom one morning, I saw one of the foxes heading home, along the garden wall. It was the dog fox; head down, and his full tail pointing down. Would he see me? He sometimes did. I knelt down and willed it, but he just dropped into the woodland, disappeared.

Their den is under the lime tree. We saw it this last spring, when the local Residents' Association spent a cold Saturday morning clearing up that little strip of embankment, bagging up cans and crisp bags, dragging rusted garden furniture free of the ivy's jealous grip. Edwyn, intrepid as ever, a boy again, worked his way to the back of our house first, and from there called me over, to look at the low arch of the foxhole. I scrambled to join him. 'Can you smell?' he said. I nodded. 'And look,' he whispered, and he pointed to a spot by the tree that we'd both seen Fox occupy. Here, amid the tangle, was a perfect oval of clear, smooth earth.

'That's where he sits when he needs a break,' I said.

Edwyn nodded seriously.

'Of course,' he said. 'Chap's got to have a break. Working so hard.'

1

Without a shift, Margaret used to spend Friday evenings with her sketchpad; lying on the settee, her long legs steepled. Conveying her character, which was thoughtful and sincere, her pale eyebrows were often drawn into a frown, looking up from her work.

I see her like that. Or maybe in her kitchen, peering mildly at her tea. Or arriving at the Pev on a rainy night: wet ragdoll, wet raincoat, wet apricot-coloured hair, poking in her purse for some jukebox change.

She was in when I got back from seeing my mother, that day at the cinema, and she looked up just as I've described, transferring her attention to the grousing figure in the doorway with unwarranted grace.

'Do you still want to go and buy a tree?' I said.

'Mmm...'

I dropped my bags on my bed and then gave my hair a brush in the hallway, while Margaret put her papers away and got on her boots and coat. She'd been letting me her box room for six months by then. I'd told myself it was a stopgap, but the truth was I didn't know how I'd ever afford to move. I didn't think about it, that was my scheme. Or else – I think I just hoped something would happen (why shouldn't it?). Margaret was away so often with her various jobs, I didn't feel too much under her feet. She said it was fine by her if I stayed on.

Pale clouds drifted over the city. Down below: wet streetlight. In Albert Square, the tree man stood in the shallows of his grove, banging his gloved hands. We moved through the spiky corridors, tried to assess the trussed-up specimens. A smallish spruce was indicated. Shoulder height. Could we lift this one? We both could, and in headlong stints we carried it home; hugging it and hoisting it, hobbling blindly forward.

Later there were nestling fairy lights, the dull glittering of Margaret's old Russian baubles, movingly fashioned after vegetables. My initiative, and a typically poor one, was tangerines stuck with cloves. These quickly ceded to rot (you were supposed to dry them out first), and within a week I was delivering them to the bin. Still – they looked nice that night, turning slowly on their threads.

Our phones were on the table with our drinks. It was about nine o'clock. I remember standing up to see who was singing, or making some kind of a lusty row, out by Napoleon's, was it? And then turning back to find my phone's message light flashing. This, as it turned out, was the 'something' happening. I read the name and felt my scalp prickle, my cheeks flush. An old circuit completed.

•

I worked in a bar while I was at university. Margaret was there too, briefly: it was where we met. And Michael Whelan – whose message I was now sitting down to read – was somebody who played there one night, in what, 2001?

Oldham Street was an outfall back then. Fuliginous nooks yielded uncertain streams of piss, on that first block of money shops, bookies, bus-stop drunks. My shift started at seven, but I'd often walk up there early, passing the smokers shivering outside the Methodist Hall, and their shadow selves, the ruined gurners who hugged the walls by the pubs, cowering in, sneering at, this new element of not-pub. Our place was handsome, in its way, with its tall windows and old theatre curtains. Posters listed WHAT'S ON in a white-on-black label-maker font: just local bands most nights, their bussed-in crowd. American musicians were unusual in that they might tip you, refusing their change with a wounded wince, a raised palm. Sometimes they'd slide over the little piles of coins they said they wouldn't take home, again turning tactfully away as you slid them into the jar. Michael did that, I think, drinking after his set. And then at the end of the night, though we'd barely talked, he said,

'I wish I could continue talking with you.'

That sullen attention. It did not waver. And the next day, too, crouching over me, whispering, with no less forcing interest.

He was twenty-eight then. I was twenty. What followed was strange. An attachment? A conviction? I make no case for it, either way. Or only this case: that it was based on nothing and fed on nothing. For the next three years we saw each other for a few days a year, that was all. Wet English winters. Black rooms above pubs. On stage, his screaming was jaw-wide. And then, afterwards, there were the strange fights he'd get into, as – he said it himself – he loved to be obnoxious. Michael was my height – short – with tightly curled brown hair, a widow's peak. He tossed his head around girlishly as he incited these set-tos, but then never looked like he was enjoying them once they got started. Rather he looked dull, resentful. His eyes in shadow; dark slots.

We used to drink a lot, together. I'd often be drunk when we met. From fear, I think.

I remember: rain like a gel on the old grey stone.

Michael saying,

'You know, *I* like it when you're like this? But *they* don't know you.'

Or in a nightclub, taking my hand, to sympathetically slur:

'I mean, I've already *been* married, so I have to be like super-careful who I *pick* next?'

Finally I started a fight, with him. We were in Derby. We argued in an eighties theme bar, then out on the street, then at a taxi rank. On it went, like promenade theatre. The year after that, he didn't call me. I knew he was in England, then Manchester. How frightening that felt. The whole city bristling with his presence (I felt), the noisy streets huzzahing his happy lack of interest in me (I felt). The years went by like that. Five years: far longer than we'd known each other.

Edwyn likes to say that 'When people are done with each other, they're done with each other.' 'People are a lot less interested in each other than you seem to *think*,' he says. I believe him now, or rather, I agree with him, but while it's hard to dispute the first proposition, its inverse does also hold. And in this case there clearly was something that I couldn't let go. Something I insisted on, for all that it crowded out.

And then came that message at Margaret's. Michael Whelan 'reaching out', as he put it. 'Seeing if this is still you.'

He wrote a little bit about what he was up to. He was living in Montana now. A town called Whitefish. 'You should look it up,' he wrote, 'it's "quaint".' He even asked if I'd mind – 'mind terribly' – sending him a copy of my new book. 'As a holiday gift for an old sweetheart?'

How strange. My mind fogged. I fell asleep quickly that night.

The next morning, too, was strange. I kept smiling helplessly, in spasms, as I walked down Oxford Road. And later, heading home, I saw a girl I knew coming towards me on her bike; just a slice of face between scarf and hat, and I raised my hand to wave to her in a way that I wouldn't have done, ordinarily.

It wasn't that I imagined myself the only one being 'reached out' to, incidentally. There was a vacancy, that's what I had to assume, and I knew him: he'd want to feel he was being fair. It didn't matter. Not to me. I replied that night, and tried to match his tone.

•

In March, Michael sent a birthday message. 'Sorry it's a little belated,' he said, 'lost track of time there!!!' I wrote: 'That's all right. Thank you. Surprised you remembered! x'

His answer to that came back like a slap.

> That felt a little sparse, coming from you – has my sporadic responsiveness agitated you?? Hope all is well in your world!!? If it's not, lemme know. Can't promise to help, but perhaps console?? Xomikey

Agitated? I thought. Console?

A phone call was my idea. At first Michael said he'd call me. But then, his phone was too shitty, he wrote, and he couldn't work his phone card? Would I mind terribly?

That was an odd conversation, full of silences I didn't care to break. Instead I held the charged little lozenge to my ear, and looked out of the window. Sackville Street at two a.m. Black and glittering.

Michael was touring again, he'd told me, in Salt Lake City that night.

'Let me just step outside,' he said, a few minutes in – to me, or to someone in the room with him.

I heard a fire door opening, then the droning wind, five thousand miles away.

'You sound cold,' I said. (I could hear the cold tightening his jaw.)

'Ya, I guess I should have put my coat on? But I'm so lazy.'

I had a can of vodka cranberry open, still wet from the fridge in

58

Spar, and I pulled on that and shivered; walked around the dark flat. The next afternoon Michael wrote to me.

Hey,

Ha ha, you were right my consolation skills were way off! I'm pretty terrible on the phone, which I do recognize is a problem in trying to be in touch with someone on another continent. Also, I DO understand your feelings concerning our relationship. I might explain to you, I am not dating anyone now but I'm also not looking/wanting to date anyone. Maybe not EVER?? Which, hey – might be similar to your feelings on the subject.

I did want to be in touch with you again because time has passed, and sure, we had a pretty awful time a few years back, but I don't believe either of us truly meant to treat each other in those ways. It was passion!! Too much of it.

But now, reaching out to you, I'm really only looking to be in touch to reconnect after all this time apart. I like the idea of being friends, which is all we can really be in our current situations anyway, right?

I hope hearing from me is a positive in your day, not another barb!! You maintain, in my memory, the most intense, confusing and frustrating experiences in my life. I mean that as sweet! And funny!!

Xomikey

People we've loved, or tried to: how to characterize the forms they assume? Michael sounded like a teenage girl, here, I thought – the queenish self-regard, the untroubled belief in his ability to coax, to blandish. That said, he didn't seem insincere, so I tried to be honest, too. I wasn't looking to 'date' him, I said. And yes, I imagined I had been quite a frustrating proposition. But there it was.

A month later he wrote again, to tell me he was playing a show in London soon. 'Too bad we're not coming to Manchester!!' he said.

'Yes, too bad,' I might have written. But I didn't do that.

At the back of the Scala people held their jackets over their arms. Drinks slopped. I left during Michael's last song, shuffling out to catch an empty bar. I took a flimsy cup of vodka to the ladies', brushed my hair out, redid it. At half past nine I walked down to the foyer. I stood and looked straight ahead while I waited. And then as we said hello, and after we'd OK'd a hug, as we were talking about what to do, where to go, I felt my eyes darting over Michael's face.

He suggested we stay and watch the next band. 'Oh,' I said. 'OK. And not talk?' That was off-putting, wasn't it? Why so jealous? So grasping, immediately? Because I knew the whole thing was hopeless? Because after all I did have a crazed and gleaming notion that it wasn't? It frightens me, to remember this. What had happened to me? What had I decided I had a right to?

Behind the bar, a muted TV screen showed the stage. Here was a singer, in white leggings and a white polo-neck, walking slowly, like a ghost in a play. Behind her a man in a black fencing outfit stood up at his drumkit. I asked if Michael knew them, were they friends? But I wasn't interested, barely listened to what he said, instead I hustled us to a pub I knew, with heedless dash, and again felt thwarted, put down, when we got there and Michael said he didn't want to get drunk. Instead he ordered a beer.

'I don't understand these. Do you want to help me out? What is that? A two pounds?'

He laid the coins out in his hand, looked at me.

Conversation was difficult. Unnatural-feeling. The attention I was paying felt like an awful kind of attention, but I didn't know how to dilute it. Michael kept needing me to repeat what I'd said, too. Sometimes because I was speaking too fast...He asked me about work, and then I asked him. He asked me what I'd been reading, and the question felt bottomlessly sad, I don't know why. I didn't tell him I'd lost my flat. I nodded when he said, 'Same place?'

His hand rested on the foot of his glass. My purse was on the table, too, ready for another round.

'So I should, um, tell you that I got engaged last year,' he said.

'OK. Goodness. Congratulations.'

'But, um...Six weeks before we were due to get married I told her that I couldn't – that I *wouldn't* – marry her.'

'OK.'

(It sounded like he'd prepared what he was saying, I remember, down to each gulping pause.)

61

'Why did you ask her?' I said.

'Oh. Um, just wanting to do right for *her*, I guess.'

'Right…' I said. 'Well…Just a sec. Sorry. Excuse me.' I stood up, edged out of the booth, heading first to the ladies' and then to the bar. What was bothering me? Making me panic? The familiarity was confounding. Michael, there in front of me. Each expression of helpless submission or bored compliance. This was him. How he passed. And living like that, of course, you would now and then end up with fiancées which had to be shaken off.

I knew more about that break-up than I let on, I should say. Guilelessly, his ex had been keeping a blog about it. Margaret and I found it after he first got in touch. A 'diary of her healing' she called it. I read it with burning cheeks at first, but that wore off. So I knew how Michael had announced, one morning, 'You know *what*? I do *not* want to marry you.' 'You are the girl that never came true!' he said, pressed for a reason. And I knew about the weekend before he moved out, when she followed him around the supermarket, begging him to reconsider. She should be grateful, he told her, that this was happening while she was still young. Still attractive enough to get someone else.

Later, scavenging, as you do, in wreckage like that, she wrote that she actually really admired the way he lived his life, citing as an example of his no-compromise attitude his turning off of the car radio one afternoon. She thought she just had to put up with bad music, but he said, 'You know *what*? I do *not* have to listen to this.' She said she'd learned from this, how she should follow *her* heart and demand the best for herself. She hadn't been doing this (she saw now) with him, turning instead to booze, pills, pot and carbs ('Cheese Bix, I'm talking to you!') to fill the emptiness when he was away on tour.

That figure echoed in our row, too.

'You know *what*? I do *not* have to be here.'

And in a story he once told me about his first summer job, at a pancake house. He decided he wanted the position, charmed the manager, then walked out on his first shift.

'You know *what*? I don't need this.'

What was this? This more-than-indignation, this self-assertion always feeling like an allegation, too. Except no one was making him do anything. Were they?

And about our argument. Too much passion, had he said? Us treating 'each other' badly? My memory was of me in great distress, behaving horribly: drunk and vicious, unrelenting, and of him scurrying away. I couldn't blame him, and that's what I'd lived with. Shame. Consequences. I believed – I believe, strongly – in both of those things. To what end, I wondered, did he think I'd want to buy in to his fiction? To a rewrite from Mr Reaching Out, Mr Reconnect? Some people will assume that we're all up for a flattering fantasy. I didn't like him, when I thought of that. So what was any of this for?

I took our drinks back to the booth, sat down. Now, after a silence, a sip, he asked me the question he always used to ask.

'So have you, um, *dated* anyone since we last…saw each other?' he said.

'Oh, no.'

'No?'

'It's not for me, you know.'

'Ya, you always said that.'

'I did. Because it's true.'

He looked at his drink, and then at the bar, impatiently. But I would have been devalued whatever I'd said. That's what I felt then. That he had a picture of me that he needed to deface. This was how he'd always proceeded, after all: reaching my periphery, meanly maundering there. (Yes, this was when it started, that night. When we both started to dig in.)

Being drunk, I decided to elaborate on what I had done in the last five years. Soon Michael had his head pressed against the wall, turning away from me, and he was chewing his thumb.

'That wasn't exactly the question, but OK.'

'What do you think happens?'

'And you couldn't wait to tell me, could you?'

He looked like a nasty little goblin then. But he was right. I had wanted to tell him. I'd always had to affect such cool around his girlfriends, fiancées, when he'd brought them up, artlessly, full of carefree, saccharine sympathy for a hurt which *I never expressed.* He felt no such compunction, clearly. I have thought, sometimes, that there should be more to getting along with people than negotiating with this jumpy primordial goo. But no – there often isn't. I back-pedalled a little.

'I just can't see myself in a couple,' I said. 'Watching box sets all night long. I can't put the hours in.'

I was being fatuous, but that was fine, as it turned out – he didn't notice, or ignored that, instead he reached across the table. Dreadful, what was about to happen. The heavy fall of the same old machinery.

'Um…Could you not see yourself, watching television – with *me*?' he said.

I looked down at his hand. I felt panic. So nor could I help what I did next, the table suddenly seeming littered with mousetraps. I drew my hand back and frowned at him. I stood and went to the bar. When I came back there was another silence. Another long look. His eyes had a different cast then, but a familiar one.

'I can't think of you…' he was saying, 'I don't think I can think of you…outside of the context of – loving you?'

This too had the air of something rehearsed. Rehearsed but deployed now accidentally, just – falling off the shelf.

Still, at midnight, a taxi. A slow ride through bouncing rain, the yellow light swimming before us. Then an off-licence near King's Cross, whose hot-pink sign said OOZE.

In his room in the Hotel Apollo I hung up my coat, sat down on the tightly made bed. I swigged from my bottle. Michael didn't want any, he'd decided, which drew another graceless frown from me. And then, while he was fiddling with the TV, asking me if I wanted to listen to some music on his phone, his 'fancy-ass new phone?' he said, I took off my clothes, pushed off my tights. I was so drunk. I sat there in my underwear and pointed out ('Hey look!')

how the fleur-de-lys pattern on the carpet matched that on my bra and knickers.

The streets looked dingy in the morning. The puddled pavements, dank guesthouses. Michael was pulling his little suitcase behind him. The wheels clicked along.

At the station, while he looked at the tube map, I shamefully said,

'When are you coming back?'

Then I said I could come to the airport with him, if he wanted?

'Oh. No,' he said, smiling blandly.

This was at King's Cross at nine a.m. Streams of people: macs, tote bags. After Michael had gone, I hunched my shoulders to push through them to the street.

On the train home I was jittery and it wouldn't abate. Sweating, head throbbing, I was also weathering another racket: that conviction I mentioned, now gorily undead, and appallingly immune to revelation. This ghastly other self kept breaking the surface of my real, frightened self, insisting scornfully that things would be fine, in fact, between Michael and me. Nothing was *instant*. Last night had been a step *forward*, in fact…

Possessed by the fact that I had to, I emailed him very early the next morning. I started by saying I was sorry that I hadn't been able to keep hold of his hand over the table. I'd felt frightened, I said, because I was in love with him, as he knew. My tone, as I recall it, reckoned itself very calm and straightforward here: as if we were just a few administrative clear-ups away from this happy new region we could attain together, after all these years of sad botching. It took him a week to write back, but long before that I realized what I'd done, and from then on I was in pain.

He began, 'Gosh, this is a lot to digest.' Then there were a lot of emphasizing capitals. I believe he wrote, 'Again, I WAS curious.' He definitely wrote, 'And YOU were clearly receptive to that also.' But the feelings I talked about weren't there for him, he said, and if I couldn't 'handle that', 'maybe it WAS a bad idea' for him to have 'reached out'.

Have I ever been as frightened as when I read that? Frightened of myself, I mean. Ashamed of how I worked. In my panic I started to reply. A letter amounting to, *Please don't cut me out.* I didn't send it. I felt afraid of my words, then, of that machine.

I left Manchester soon afterwards. I moved out while Margaret was away; didn't stay to say goodbye as we'd planned. I just dropped the key in her letterbox and went. Befitting what I was.

2

Glasgow, I barely knew. I'd stayed overnight before; walked through the drizzling dark from the station to the bookshop, from the bookshop to the hotel. Now, trying to find a flat, I spent four nights in a Travelodge, rode the subway, talked to letting agents. Neighbourhoods, areas began to mean something, up and down Great Western Road. I ate my lunch back in my room every day, scrolling through Gumtree, calling numbers I'd seen in shop windows. At night I walked the wide streets quickly, arms folded. My way into life was the same.

I took a lease on the first place I liked, which was in Partick, in a tenement opposite the infirmary. From my small, square hallway, doors opened to the bedroom at the back and the living room at the front. The kitchen was a nook, behind a folding vinyl door, and the bathroom was a narrow cut; you had to squeeze into the shower, elbows tucked: a saint in its niche. The place had the feel of an old B&B, I thought, or rooming houses I'd read about: the knotty carpet, cane furniture; the souvenir coasters in the cutlery drawer.

My landlords were my neighbours: Mark and Mary Bowles, a brother and sister in their fifties. They were also custodians of a huge cat, Kit-Kat, whose habit it was, most afternoons, to slip out of their living room and make her way to my place. Three floors up, she'd step along the rust-coloured stones, rounding the corner to my bathroom, whose window she could further open with a paw-push, a headbutt, before decanting herself onto the cistern, then onto the toilet seat.

I rarely saw Mary, but Mark was always around: sweeping the stairs every morning, first with a broom, then getting into the corners with a small plastic brush. The walls were tiled to waist height out there, with bottle-green bricks. He'd sponge them down, carefully carrying his steaming bowl of suds between the landings. After a blowy night, I'd see him retrieving any bin lids that had been scattered around the courtyard. With a spool of hairy twine and a pair of kitchen scissors, he'd retie each one to its parent. When he wasn't working, I might pass him on the house's front step, where it was his pleasure to stand and smoke, catching the ash in a little anchovy jar. Whatever the weather, he wore a tight, stripy polo-shirt, and blue jeans, and fleece-lined Crocs.

I just had my clothes and my laptop. In the fridge were the vegetables that I cooked in the evening; in the cupboard, a jar of tahini and a bag of sunflower seeds, for protein. My cleanser and my toothpaste and toothbrush were wedged behind the taps of the tiny bathroom sink.

If I walked into town, it was to Waterstone's, or to Holland &
Barrett, for teabags. Back at home I lay on the bed and read, while
outside the wind roamed. Seagulls fell. Sleep swept me up, that
first summer. Sleep and lazing, with Kit-Kat. Later, when I got a
job up there, in a fancy soap shop, I found it difficult, at first, to
talk to people.

In fact, any urge for contact fell away, really, for a while. I was
my own. Quiet.

Only very rarely would restlessness have me leave the flat at
night, and usually the impulse could be quitted by buying a bottle
in the Costcutter and heading home again. The current of night life
on Dumbarton Road was only old men walking back from the pub:
bow-legged, in glossy blazers, flapping jeans. Lying on my bed, feeling my face and mind warmed over, it wasn't the stab of loneliness
that ebbed away, but the idea that there was any cure for it out there.
I read. I worked on a novel. And then weeks might go by before I'd
find myself trotting down the stairs again. To hang on bars. To feel
a rising panic, no matter how I held my head up.

Stevie Gillies, at work, was one friend I made. He was funny. An
unillusioned person. I used to sit with him while he wrote emails
to his son, in the internet café under his flat; The Lite Byte, a seedy
place, selling coffee and powdered soup, its walls covered in peach
bathroom tiles. I'd go with Stevie in his van some nights, too, when
he was doing his other job, a delivery job.

One morning, as we were leaving for our Saturday shift, I found a
postcard on my doormat. One of those kitsch postcards: repurposed

photographs. This one featured an old lady from the seventies, with a cauliflower perm and garish make-up. She was wearing a cleaner's tabard and wielding a duster, camply. *'Get in Touch or I'm Coming to Visit!'* said the caption, and on the back my mother had written: *Only joking!!! Mum.* I passed it to Stevie, while I locked the door, and he read it and handed it back. I was going to reply, send an email maybe, but before we'd even got to the shop that day, she texted me:

CUT ALL MY HAIR OFF DO YOU WANT BRUSH AND BOBBLES
ETC. MUM

At lunchtime I phoned her, from a quiet bit of the arcade.
'What's going on?'
'Oh, nothing. Nothing's going on, Neve.'
'You've had a haircut?'
'Oh, yes, I have. I've cut it all off. But try telling Rodger that! I was sitting there having tea with him and I said, Er, notice anything different, hey? Ahem, ahem. No. Nothing. "What are you talking about?" But then he never looked at me before, did he, so why should he notice now, I suppose? So yes, I thought, I've got this *hairbrush* now that I don't need and these bobbles, so...'
'I have got my own hairbrush, thanks.'
'OK, well. I'll keep them, then, anyway. I won't throw them out.'
'Everything OK otherwise?'
'Well. *No*, Neve, not really.'
'What's going on?'

'Well, I did…The night *after* that business with the haircut, we were having tea, and I did say then, because I've been thinking, and it is all a bit much lately, so I did say, to Rodger, *Well*, Neve's moved and it's *so exciting*, a new city, and it's made me think *I'd* like to move now, try somewhere new, so yes, I did say then that I was thinking I *might* move out.'

'What did he say to that?'

'Oh, he just went mad. Absolutely mad. *But* – I was prepared, so…You know I've been making this list, well, you don't know, but I have, of things he does that I don't like, or, you know, not very nice things, and it ran to three pages in the end! So I did show him that.'

'You showed him?'

'*Yes*. And oh, he went mad. He just said – Out. Get out. So I went straight upstairs then and started looking at flats on Right-move. But he has lifted that sentence now, so…I can go in my own time. But yes, I am going now.'

'That's good.'

'Yes. Well. I think it's just…I'd had enough, really!'

'Where will you go?'

'Well, I don't *know*. All my activities are in Liverpool, but then he says that's over now. None of his friends would want to stay my friend, apparently, so I'm to be ostracized, you see, he says, my name's going to be mud, apparently, so…*Persona non grata*.'

'That's nice.'

'Well, that's what he says. Anyway, I'd like to move to Manches-ter, I think.'

'Really?'

'Yes. I *love* Manchester, Neve.'

'OK. You've got a plan, then, you can start looking for somewhere.'

'I'm already looking. I've looked at lots of places.'

'Great. Well, I'm out and about, so I should probably go. Are you coming to visit or was that an idle threat?'

'Well, I thought I *could*. I thought, I love Glasgow *so much*, and I am *retired* now so why not take advantage, having a *daughter* who lives there…'

'Why not take advantage.' Words to live by. I turned off my phone and thought about crossing the precinct to slot it down the grid outside Zara, or maybe dismantling it, dropping the pieces in the three different bins I could see: a discreet disposal, before I went back to the shop.

As it turned out, it was a while before I heard from my mother again. She went quiet. Went dark. I got a parcel at Christmas. When she did start calling, in spring, I didn't pick up at first. I'm not often in the frame for her attentions (I imagine my brother bears the brunt) but with Rodger potentially off the scene back then, I felt I had to be careful.

She left a message in the end. '*Now*,' she said, 'I've finally got a *gap in my schedule*, so…'

3

Blobs of rain shivered on the Plexiglas. I looked down at Mark about his labours, pegging washing on a carousel, and Kit-Kat on the wall, and a seagull despoiling a binbag. That courtyard was like a well, or a sea cave; slathered in wet green moss. My mother was due. She was getting a taxi from the station.

She arrived with her usual cargo. Two William Morris tote bags, which I took off her on the stairs, leaving her with her plump old handbag, and her yellow shoulderbag, in plastic made to look like wicker. Across her body was a turquoise sports bag, and further to these panniers, she held a Boots plastic bag in her right hand, and a paper bag in her left: her half-eaten sandwich from the train. She was staying for two nights. I stood by the door as she stepped into the flat, as she bared her teeth and crept forward. This was my home, and I was letting her into it. I'd never done that before. I haven't since. It gave me a strange feeling. Revulsion, I suppose you'd have to call it.

I put her luggage in the bedroom, and then admired her coat, which was purple, bell-shaped, with large white buttons.

'Oh, do you like it? It's "mod", isn't it? Do you know, I bought it online because it was just *so* reduced, but it wasn't until it came that I saw it said "Do not get wet" on the label, so I haven't been able to wear it all winter! This is the first time I've dared put it on! Of course it's too warm now! I don't know!'

Purple is my mother's 'favourite colour' and that day her nails were painted magenta and her lipstick was a shimmering mauve. Under her coat she wore a purple jumper and brown checked ski-pants. The shoes were an old pair of mine. I used to wear them to school.

'Have they not fallen apart?'

'Oh, no. No. And they're back in now!'

That first evening we walked up to Byres Road, to a Greek restaurant. My mother took it all in excitedly: the clipped-on paper tablecloths and the blue-and-white striped placemats, the mock vine creeping over the bar. The wall behind her was painted like a vase: a train of callipygian swains, with blunt beards and beetle brows. She twisted around to look up at them.

'Oh dear!' she said.

'Is this a *regular haunt*, then?' she said, smoothing out her napkin.

'No. I've never been here. I've just been past. I don't eat out, I'm poor.'

'Oh. Well. Looks nice, anyway, doesn't it?'

She picked up the menu.

'Lots of things you can eat,' she said. 'Houmous.'

'Yep.'

She'd stuck with her new hairstyle. It was quite severe: a crop, with a saw-tooth fringe. She kept touching the back of her neck, kept trying to tuck two little darts of hair behind her ears.

'I don't know what these are,' she said. 'They don't listen, do they, when you go in.'

When we both knew what we wanted, she tried to catch a waiter's eye. She didn't have much luck, but kept grinning, lifting her chin. I said,

'So you're single now.'

'Yes, yes, I am. Single lady. Well, *separated*.'

'Congratulations.'

'Oh. Yes. Well. Thank you!'

'How long were you with him, in the end? Was it ten years?'

'Yes. Now. Neve. Shall we just catch him, while he's in the vicinity?'

She lifted her hand up, showed her teeth. A tall waiter came and crouched by the table. He spoke to her indulgently, as if she were much older than she was, and she smiled back at him happily, nervously, as we both gave our orders.

'Was it ten years?' I said, as he left.

'Well, yes, it is ten years now, just about…Yes, I was *fifty*-two when I married him, so…Yes, I remember thinking, Well, that's that, then, winding down. I don't know. Fifty-two seems young now, now that I'm *sixty*-two!'

'He just turned nasty, did he?'

'Yes, he just…Yes, he did turn. I thought, Do I want to spend my life with this miserable old man, really? He never wanted to do anything or go anywhere.'

'You two were always going out.'

'Yes, I *know*, but I had to organize that, you see. That was all down to me. I had to sort of corral him into that. And then when he was going out with *his* mates, I wasn't invited. He'd say, I'm going for a drink, and I'd say, Ahem, am *I* not invited, then? And, no, I wasn't.'

'But you're out of the house now?'

'Yes, of course. I've been out nearly two months now, Neve! And what I've done is I've rented a little place in Manchester, in the "Green Quarter", it's called, do you know it?'

'I don't think so. In the city centre?'

'Yes. In Ancoats, is it? It's on Newton Street. It used to be a post office.'

'Oh, yes. But that's a party building, isn't it?'

'What's that?'

'People having parties.'

'Is it? Not in my flat! It can get noisy. It's very nice, though. "Landscaped Japanese gardens", as the website says. It's just like all these modern places, really, quite cramped and bare, but it's just temporary. I'm looking for somewhere to buy. A little sort of *bachelorette pad*. Rodger is quite insistent now, that I have to get my things out, finally, so he's going to go away this weekend and I'm going to go and box everything up. I don't think I'll bother with storage. It's very expensive, isn't it, I mean, how do you manage?'

'I don't really. I should sort it out.'

'Yes, so I'll just get a *man with a van* and have him stack them in the flat until I find somewhere permanent. If there's room! I've got so much stuff!'

'Did you two have another showdown or did you just clear off?'

'Yes, I just cleared off, really. Just sort of found this place online and went. Oh, but people are so funny about it. I was on a church tour with the Vic Soc last weekend and there were various people saying, Ooh, where's Rodger? And so I said, *Well*, we're not together any more, and my friend Marianne just burst out crying! And John Quinn, this very nice *gay* man, he said, Oh, I could tell you two weren't happy. I thought, Could you?'

'I think you could. I didn't like being around you. It looked like a vaudeville act.'

'Ooh, a vaudeville act, what's that? Well. Anyway, I've written to Eric and said, Yes, we are *separated* now. I sent him an email, so…'

'Oh, yes. What does Eric say?'

'Well, I've not heard back from him *yet*, but I think he's very busy trying to sell his house, so…'

'Did you ever clarify his situation?'

'Not really. I mean, he did make this surprise announcement last year that he had this girlfriend in *Windsor*, you see, but he hasn't mentioned her since, and I've never met her. He's often at these Vic

GWENDOLINE RILEY

Soc dos and she's never with him, so when do they see each other, hey? Anyway, as I say, he's moving to London in September, he's a visiting professor or something...'

She looked dubious, wrinkled her nose.

'It's great that you're so interested in his work,' I said.

She went on:

'Yes. So last time I saw him, I was asking him about this flat he's found down there, and he drew me a floorplan, you see. Here's the kitchen. Here's the sitting room. And *then*, in the bedroom he drew this little rectangle, and he said, And this is my single bed. So I felt like saying, Oh, well, what do you do when your *girlfriend* comes to stay? But I didn't, I just said, Oh. And then I said I was thinking of coming to London in the new year, to see some exhibitions, hint hint, and did he say I could stay at his place? No. Nothing. Or maybe go for dinner? No.'

'He'd just told you that his flat only had one bedroom and a single bed.'

'Well. Yes. But. You'd think he'd say, Oh, if you need somewhere to stay, or if you want someone to show you around.'

'You've lived in London. Why would he show you around? And you're an adult, and you're solvent, what's wrong with a hotel? I don't think you should pin all your hopes on this man. It doesn't sound like there are sparks flying.'

'Oh, yes, yes, there are. We have terrific *badinage*. What do you mean? What do you mean, pin all my hopes?'

'You know what I mean.'

80

'No, I don't actually. Now here's our food, is it? Yes.'

She sat back and lifted her hands, smiled up at the waiter.

I went on:

'I just mean, if either of you wanted something to happen, it would have happened, wouldn't it? And he's fifty-two, and you're sixty-two. That's a big difference for a man his age.'

'Yes, I *know*. This girlfriend in Windsor is thirty-five, apparently.'

'And you've told me before you don't fancy him.'

'Oh, no, I *don't* fancy him. Not at all.'

'And you're not interested in sex.'

'No, I'm not. Yuck. But I just – I don't know. I just would like it if, you know, if he needed a plus one for an event that could be me…'

'I see. But what events are these?'

'Oh, I don't know. Dinners, or…I don't know. He goes to lots of these dinners with his work. Functions and things.'

'If you aren't his girlfriend, I'm not sure how you could finesse that. If you'd like to meet up in London, why can't you say that? I think you should be straightforward rather than trying to contrive something. Men don't pick up on those things.'

'No. Well, *he* doesn't. I mean, in that email I sent him I said I was moving out and oh, what a nightmare it would be, getting my suitcases from the taxi to the train and then up all these stairs to this new flat, because you have to *cross* these Japanese gardens to get to it, and did he write back and say he'd drive me over, in his nice big car? No. I just could *not* have been dropping a bigger hint.'

81

'Well, there you go, then. People can't be bothered with other people's dramas. And you've got money to pay someone! Why try and insinuate yourself like this?'

'Well, I don't know,' she said. 'As a *friend*, he might have thought it would be nice to offer...'

While we ate I asked her about all of her clubs: the 'Vic Soc', the Wine Circle, the Clan Grant Society. She was keeping up with all of them, without Rodger. I asked about my brother, whether he'd seen our father.

'Oh, no. He's been to see Rodger, though. Apparently Rodger says, You'll *always* be my stepson. So...'

I asked her if she'd been to the pictures recently, then told her what I'd been to see. She held her hands in fists while I was talking, and bared her teeth.

'Well, you'll *never* guess what I've been having for tea,' she said, 'in my new, single life! Oh, it's awful. I just have a can of lager and a huge bag of Kettle Chips! Oh, or Bombay mix. I just had a tub of Bombay mix last night!'

'That's really bad for you.'

'I *know*.'

'I mean, you needn't have a meal, but you need nutrients.'

'Yes, I *know*.'

'What's wrong with vegetables? Just buy some green beans or some broccoli. They only take a couple of minutes to cook. Vegetables, and some seeds, for protein.'

'*Mmm*...But I just can't be bothered!' she said, happily. And then, in a teenager's whine, switching her pigeon-chick head from side to side: *'Can't be bothered,'* she said. *'Cannot. Be. Bothered.'*

After dinner we walked back down Dumbarton Road towards my flat. We stopped in at the Three Judges – my idea – where my mother asked for another large glass of white wine. The table we took was on a platform by the window. As I brought over the drinks she was gazing out hungrily, hands on the sill like a child waiting for snow.

'It's lively around here, isn't it?' she said. 'Do you come in here a lot?'

'No, not really. Sometimes.'

'I think I came in here with Rodger last time,' she said. 'You know we came up for the Charles Rennie Mackintosh weekend? Well, we did, and I think we came in here, because we were staying in a hotel quite near here. Well, a guest house, really. Did I ever tell you about that? Oh, God, it was awful. Rodger went *mad.*'

'Did he? Go on.'

'Well, we'd all been out, with Dennis and Sarah, and yes, I think we came here, and just, drinking and drinking, and then sort of rolled back to this guest house, where Rodger *got fresh*, you see.'

'Got fresh?'

'Yes. Just. You know. So I *rebuffed* him, you see. I said just, "Oh. No." And then he just went mad. Absolutely mad. He said the material of my nightdress was *disgusting*. Yes, that was it: *"The material of your nightdress is disgusting."* And then he said, "It's all right for you, you can pleasure yourself.'"

'What does that mean?'

'Well, I don't *know*.'

'Did you ever have sex, Mum?'

She shook her head, screwed up her eyes.

'Oh, no. No. But, Neve, it gets worse! It gets worse!'

'Go on.'

'He said he'd seen me masturbating in the garden!'

'OK.'

'Well, it's a strip of *concrete*, really. Our "terrace", I used to call it. He said he'd seen me out there on the sun lounger pleasuring myself!'

'Pleasuring yourself?'

'Well, masturbating, you see.'

'You were masturbating?'

'No! Neve! I don't know what on *earth* he thought he'd seen!'

'Perhaps that's what he wanted to see.'

'Ooh, is it? Do you think?'

'Of course. It's a fantasy. Keep up. Shall we go back now? Is that finished?'

'Oh. Yes. Nearly. Sorry, Neve,' she said, face flushed, gulping down the last of her drink.

She was taking the bed, and I was sleeping in the living room, on the settee. I turned over the cushion where Kit-Kat liked to roll about, smudged as it was with little tufts of her black hair.

•

My mother came knocking very early in the morning. A timid knock, first, then she pushed the door open, peeped in, then stepped in.

'Neve? Neve?'

I sat up, pulling the blanket up with me.

'What do you want?'

'Oh, nothing. Nothing, Neve.'

She had on her long nightdress, and her hair was fluffed-up. She bared her teeth and looked around the room, then shyly back at me. She took another step forward. She had her fleecy bedsocks on, too: baby pink with a fluffy cuff. (These were called 'Dozy Toes'. There'd been two pairs in my Christmas parcel.)

'Oh, are you nudie, Neve?' she said.

'What?'

'Do you sleep in the nudie?'

'Sometimes.'

'Ooh, doesn't it feel funny? Oh, I could never sleep in the nudie!'

'What do you want?'

'Nothing. Just, seeing if you were up, so…I'll make some tea, shall I? Do you have tea? I don't know if I can work that kettle!'

We went out for breakfast instead. In the Big Mouth Café she opened the magazine that came with the newspaper.

'Are you a *feminist*, Neve?' she said.

'Yes, I'd hope so. Why?'

'Well, we're all feminists now, apparently.'

'OK.'

She had before her a spread about some activists.

'I don't know,' she said. 'They're so against men, aren't they, but half of them look like men!'

'Do they?'

'Well, I don't know. Don't you think?'

When we swapped our bits of the paper she started huffing about the front page, which featured another old entertainer charged with sexual assault. An archive picture showed the accused in a red jumper, grinning and doing an OK sign. Next to it was a shot of him on the court steps: sour-faced. My mother didn't see the point of any of this. Back in the seventies every girl was gripped, groped and raped, said she, lifting her chin, her accent getting coarser (you heard it on the *r*s).

'I was raped, when I was at university, I was more or less raped in Liverpool when I first moved back. It didn't ruin my life. Why do they always have to say, Ooh, it ruined my life? And *everything* I went through with your father, I mean, if that didn't ruin my life, why are they saying their lives are ruined?'

'Strange, isn't it?' I said.

I was more interested, in that same conversation, to hear, apropos of a friend of mine who was expecting, that my mother had had terrible panic attacks in the weeks before I was born. I didn't know that. Twice my father called an ambulance, apparently. My mother couldn't breathe.

What was she so frightened of?

'The pain, of course! I was sick with fear!'

Just that? Maybe. I think she must have known she'd invited a reckoning – one she'd dodge, naturally, but that wouldn't have forestalled the terror, would it?

I'm very glad my mother left my father, of course, but as I got older it did get harder to valorize that flight. This cover-seeking – desperate, adrenalized – had constituted her whole life as far as I could see. In avoidance of any reflection, thought. In which case her leaving him was a result of the same impulse that had had her hook up with him in the first place. Not to think, not to connect: marry an insane bully. Simper at him. Not to be killed: get away from him. And her children? Her issue? How did they fit into her scheme? As sandbags? Decoys?

Perhaps I should be more moved by her than I am. I love animals, their natural ways. I have asked her about my – our – childhood, that house, but you wouldn't think I'd spoken. She just stared back at me. Maybe she never noticed what we grew up with. Left to herself, back there, as I'm sure she felt she was, she laced the fetid air with her high-pitched humming, her little self-announcements:

'Well, I'm going to sit in the *sun lounge* if anyone wants me. Do they? No.'

'Well, *I'm* going to eat some *strawberries and cream* and watch *Wimbledon*. Yes.'

My brother was even more incensed by these notices than I.

'*Do I give a shit?*' he'd scream.

You couldn't see the television if the curtains were open, so they never were open. She'd clear a space on the settee and hold up by her chest her bowl of mushy frozen strawberries, topped with spray cream. She lifted her chin, bared her teeth.

I tried to lie there with her once, when I was small. She didn't like it, I could tell, but I didn't get down. *Ski Sunday*, was she watching? Or a Grand Prix? I took a chance, made another move: I held her clenched bare foot and kissed it.

'Oh. *No*, Neve.'

She struggled to pull away.

'No. Don't do that,' she said, looking fearful, then angry. She pulled her knees up by her chest. 'That's like what a…*boyfriend* would do,' she said. 'Not your *daughter. No.*'

She got married again a year after my brother moved out. I sat and watched her smirk her way through those vows. A wriggly performance. And he was no better, I might say.

Then began her leering pleas: '*Do* come and visit, Neve. You've got a lovely *home* here now.' I went once, to that house, in Aigburth. I went for help, because I was desperate, after that final break with Michael. Margaret was away, and anyway I felt too ashamed to tell my friends what had happened. It is strange what we expect from people, isn't it? Deep inside ourselves. As adults. I was crying and she bared her teeth at me, like a cretin. I had to run. I took my bag, my coat. Only she wouldn't let me leave. She blocked my way at the front door and screamed for Rodger. She was looking over my shoulder and shrieking out his name.

'Rodger! Help! Rodger! She's gone mad!'

All through that marriage, if I asked how she was, I got her itinerary, read out from the long-leaved kitchen calendar, if we were on the phone, or else from the little diary she scrabbled for in her bag:

'Yes, so, Wednesday's the Wine Circle, isn't it? And then the Vic Soc on *Friday*…'

And all in that doll's-tea-party voice: self-enclosed, self-chivvying. She was very keen to share her programme that day in the café, too, opening the slim appointment book on her knee, smiling down at the week's activities.

'Now where are we? Wednesday, yes. Look at this. Every day I've got something on. I never stop!'

'You need to stay in more.'

'I know! It's hysteria, Neve! Hysteria and desperation! I panic if I've got nothing on. But there's all sorts on in *Manchester*, isn't there? This *art* opening at the Whitworth I'm going to, see, so…'

'Does anyone talk to you when you're at these dos?'

'No! Well, no one new. I stand there "looking approachable" all night! But no one approaches! No one. No. There *are* people I know from the Vic Soc. But yes, I would…yes, I do just need some mates now, so…I mean, I *did* ask, when I first moved into this place, I did ask some people from the Vic Soc round for, you know, *flat-warming nibbles* and *drinks*, and some people came, but you would think, wouldn't you, that, you know, *I* might get an invitation in return. *Nothing.* Not one.'

She went on:

'But I said that to *Eric*, actually, when I first met him. You know, I invited him out for a Christmas meal with, you know, *Rodger* and Sylvia and her husband, and he said, "I seem to have been promoted to the top table rather quickly!" So I just said, '*No*, actually.' And I told him that I'd looked around at my sixtieth and there wasn't *one* person I could phone up and go to the pictures with or for coffee with, so...'

'But that's an interesting insight, isn't it? Why do you think that is?'

'Well...Why do I think what is? What d'you mean?'

'Why do you think you don't have any friends you can meet up with?'

'Oh, never mind meet up with. You know I broke my *ankle* the first week I was in that flat?'

'No, I didn't know.'

'Well, I *did*. I just fell off the pavement. Thankfully a *very* nice man did come and help me, and called an ambulance for me, but after that I had this plaster cast on for two weeks. Well, it was like a big ski boot, really, but it was removable, for when I went to bed or if I wanted to get in the bath. You had to keep it dry, you see, so when I went down to get my mail in the morning I had to put a Tesco bag over it, so...Not very pleasant! But I had that on when I had this flat-warming. You'd think, wouldn't you, that people would say, Oh, are you all right, what have you done? Not one person

– well, one person asked but only so she could tell the story of *her* injury – and then John Quinn, who I'm quite friendly with, actually, he came over and asked how I was and I said, Well, I've broken my *ankle*, John, and he said, Oh, and then – not, How did you do that? Or, How are you managing? Just, Oh – and then asked me what time we were finishing! So...'

'How did you manage?'

'Well, Tesco *do* deliver, luckily. But of course I still had to trek out across these gardens to meet them at the foyer, because it's *such* a labyrinth. But after two weeks of that they gave me another cast with a sort of Velcro sandal on the bottom, so, yes, I was able to get out and about a bit more then, go to openings and things, but, yes...That came off a month ago now, but I still have all these exercises I'm supposed to do...'

'Have you thought any more about getting therapy?'

'Oh. No. Not yet, I mean...'

I'd pursued this line with her before, though I'm not sure why. It was a perverse idea, really.

'If you want to live a more fulfilled life, it can be helpful,' I said.

'What do you mean? I do lead a fulfilled life! I lead a *very* fulfilled life!'

'I mean, if you feel disappointed, or stuck. Not able to connect with people. Lots of people have therapy. It doesn't mean you're mad.'

'*You* were mad,' she said, after a moment, quickly, and with a sort of – *There!*

91

'OK. Look. You said yourself it was hysteria, your not being able to stay in. And you just said you don't have friends. All this darting about...'

'Darting about? I am not darting about. I am *not*. I'm starting a *new life* in Manchester!'

'But you aren't making friends. Therapy might help you relate to people.'

'I know how to relate to people. I know more than *you*. Don't you dare say that. I...'

'Doesn't sound like it.'

'I think we'd better end this conversation now, Neve, before I get annoyed.'

'Fine. But you come across as very needy. Just so you know. If you want to be friends with Eric, or anybody, then you can't just keep putting yourself in their way and expecting them to pick you up.'

'What do you mean, pick me up? What's that, "Pick me up"? Needy? Oh, no, I'm not needy. I'm too far the other way, if anything. I'm *completely* the other way. *That's* probably what's put him off.'

The day stretched before us. It was barely midday. We went to the Kelvingrove Gallery next and looked at the Glasgow Style exhibition. This was my mother's idea, although she'd seen it several times before, she told me, indignantly. We went around together; stood together before a green glass door panel, a dimpled copper kettle; we walked around a walnut screen, took in a light fitting that looked like a pagoda. Finally, we wandered through a reconstructed lunchroom, read the old menus.

Afterwards, in the tea shop, my mother's subject, somehow, was the little boat her father had bought and refurbished when she was a teenager.

'*Well…*' she said, spreading some jam on a scone:

'He saw an advert in the *Wirral Globe*, you see. An *old ship's lifeboat* for sale in Birkenhead. So he phoned up and said he'd like to have a look at it, and I went with him that Saturday, only he didn't dare ring the doorbell at first! We'd parked around the corner, and he was *so* shy, we just walked past the house a few times while he worked himself up to it. Only *then*, you see, I saw this group of men coming the other way, walking up from the station! A big gang of them: long hair, flares, and I just knew, I just *knew*, they were there to look at the boat and I said, "Dad, Dad, come on!" So we did go and knock on the door then, and had a look at this upside-down boat in the garden, and luckily the couple who owned it were *very* friendly and although my dad didn't want to say yes, *then*, they did say they'd give him first refusal, which was lucky because I was right, and just then the doorbell rang and it *was* those men I'd seen, and they were all students from the University of Liverpool, you see, and they wanted this boat to do up for their Sailing Society. And they were dead keen. Well. My dad *agonized* but Mum and I just *begged* him to get it, so he did phone up again and said, Yes, please, I'll take it, so then we drove over there with the trailer and brought it home. And that was their project for the summer then, my mum and dad. He gutted the whole thing and put a cabin in, and a little kitchen. He was *so* ingenious. *So* resourceful, using bits from around the house, or the garage. He was an *extraordinary* man. It's *such* a shame he died so young.

'And then your grandma took over and she put Fablon on everything, on the tabletop and the cupboards, and she had three mugs and she put Fablon on them, too, and she sewed these long foam cushions for the benches, in matching colours.

'So that was what we did every holiday then. We went *all over*, but I did wonder, I mean, operating those locks, it was so stressful, every time! And there always seemed to be people waiting or people who'd just *stare* from the towpath and he'd get terribly anxious, you know, sweating and clenching his jaw. I don't know why he put himself through it. Oh, but the worst was when we took it to Wales. He was determined to go out to sea but we got stuck in the bay! In *Colwyn* Bay. And of course all of these locals lined up along the harbour wall to watch us, all these hairy Welsh villagers, shaking their heads at this family on their gaff-rigged dinghy. But he wouldn't turn back! Mum and I were just pleading with him, just *begging* him to turn back. She wrote one of her poems about that for the *Reader's Digest*. You know she was mad for entering their competitions? Well, she was. She didn't win but she was always *placed*. They were great competitions because they gave you a different rhyme scheme each time, and how many syllables, and this one you had to repeat certain lines. Let me remember.'

She sat up straighter. She lifted her hands off the table, spread her fingers.

'One more starboard tack should do it!
Out of the harbour and into the sea.
Taken aback! We'll never get through it!
One more starboard tack should do it.

One more starboard tack should do it!
Though wind and waves de da de dum
The local dum de dum, "They'll rue it!"
One more starboard tack should do it.

One more starboard tack should do it!'

'OK, OK. No more starboard tacks, please. Jesus.'

'Well, I can't remember any more! But it went on, you get the idea…Let me remember another one.'

'Please don't. I don't like it. I'm serious.'

Again she sat up, preened a little.

'*Now*,' she said, and she lifted her hands and framed her face with her thumbs and index fingers.

"It's raining again," said my mother
Flinging the curtains wide
"The police have come for your brother
And the last of the roses have died."'

'Horrible,' I said. 'I told you to stop.'

'Yes, I *know*,' she said, happily.

4

God help me. Days after she left, that voice was still tripping around my mind. When I lay down to sleep I heard her yapping and thought I really would go mad. What to do? Deep breaths? I stroked Kit-Kat's little paws, when she'd let me, until she stretched out a paw to stop me, and I walked in to the shop and back every day at a sort of dazzled double-speed.

The mornings were dreary, the wind warm and low. Sometimes in the evenings came an almost-rain, scratching at the air.

I worked when I got home. I let things drift with Stevie.

Finally, in late June, a phone call I was pleased to receive: the brisk, purling voice of one Maureen at Scottish Arts. I'd won a fellowship, seven weeks in France, starting – now, more or less. 'Oh, yes, you had best get packing!' she said.

I pulled my holdall from under the bed while she filled in the details.

5

A cheque. That felt nice. I could hold myself differently. The Kings Cross Inn took the first tranche of that stipend: a double room, on the seventh floor, with a long view of the Euston Road.

I fell asleep with the curtains open, after an evening of doing sit-ups, drinking water, then soaking in the deep, old bath.

When I woke up, the sun was panelling the walls, the bed. There was the hollow tok-tok of construction work on the other side of the street and some slightly scrambled-sounding disco coming from the workmen's radio. I opened the window, as far as I could, set the bath running again, filled up the kettle.

The light felt forgiving, and just to prove this was so, I decided to write to Michael Whelan. I lay poking at my Blackberry, saying that I'd just woken up and was sorry about everything. *I hope you don't mind my writing*, I wrote (adopting, it occurs to me, something of his off-key politesse: that was weird, but then I was in a weird mood, clearly. A mad mood.)

•

In the stone-clad breakfast room I had a black coffee and a cup of dry muesli. I think my fellow guests were all bound for the Eurostar, too. Here were anxious, scrubbed couples, an American family in their easeful travelling clothes. The table next to mine was empty, its raspberry-coloured cloth covered in cup rings and pastry scraps. They had left a paper, though. I took that and tried to find a weather forecast.

My train arrived late at Bourron Marlotte and I walked quickly through the cool brick passage to the car park, half-afraid that there'd be no one there to meet me. My phone was dead, I didn't know what I'd do in that case. Were there phone boxes in France? In the middle of France, or wherever I was? But my host was there, unbothered, standing by her hatchback and smoking. She was all in white: white tunic, capri pants. Her hair was grey-brown and cut in a chin-length bob. Smiling hello, dropping her cigarette, she shook my hand, said, 'I am Laurine,' then pointed at the back seat for my bag. It was just a short drive to where I'd be staying and Laurine drove fast. Her little feet on the pedals were sun-toasted, crinkly, with a pearly polish on the nails. I opened the window and felt the warm wind on my face.

'Now,' said Laurine, nodding to the front door of the villa.

She held up a set of keys and shook them, jingle-jingle, like a cat's bell.

'This one. And. Patient, patient, patient…'

We walked through a long, shadowy sitting room. Here were faded kilims, empty fruit bowls. Outside a team of gardeners were seeing to the lawn, and through patio doors came the tomatoey smell of cut grass, and the scorched smell of hot machinery. Silver-blue stripes trailed down to a riverbank.

'Y a-t-il d'autres personnes ici?' I said.

'Ah oui, bien sûr. Des peintres suédois. De Göteborg, je crois. Ils sont ici depuis le début d'été. Ils se trouvent dans le studio tous les jours si vous voulez y aller les voir, ou…Il y a deux hommes, une femme. Ils partent dans une semaine, et après cela, il n'y aura que vous dans la maison.'

'Des artistes-peintres? Bien.'

I never did meet them. They looked so young. I saw them out on the lawn one day, cutting loose with a beanbag.

I worked in the library. The sun reached my chair at two, and then my words blazed and my eyes winked. I spent the afternoons reading in my room, testing my French on the classics I'd found:

La petite ville de Verrières peut passer pour l'une des plus jolies de la Franche-Comté. OK. *Ses maisons blanches avec leurs toits pointus…*

The wood-pigeons gathered on my windowsill, and theirs were the only sounds I heard. Their hoo-hoo. Their fussy wing-slaps, like rifled cards.

I walked for an hour or so each day, after I'd finished my work.

The streets were empty then. Here was: weathered stone. A ruined keep. At the edge of the village the lamp posts had been fitted out with sandwich boards, advertising the circus.

Michael's reply, when it came, wasn't unfriendly. It was toneless. It was like it was done with mirrors, I remember thinking, or realizing, during one of those walks, offering no advance on an image of my own angst, sort of trapped there. 'Sounds like things are going pretty great with you!!' he'd written. I shrank at that. Still, being abroad, at least, being out of it somehow, I found it was possible to feel less implicated. Less accounted for. And finally, climbing the stairs one evening, hanging my bag on a chair: unaccounted for.

III

1

Considering one's life requires a horribly delicate determination, doesn't it? To get to the truth, to the heart of the trouble. You wake and your dreams disband, in a mid-brain void. At the sink, in the street, other shadows crowd in: dim thugs (they are everywhere) who'd like you never to work anything out.

About six months after I moved in: it was cold out, raining. The candle was lit, flying its pale flag, and in the row of houses opposite, all the windows were dark. All of our little theatres.

'It's quite lonely round here in the evenings, isn't it?' I said. 'No one's ever in over there. And that must be fifteen flats.'

Edwyn swallowed his mouthful, smiled at me, briefly. He had his blue cardigan on over a grey T-shirt, with the sleeves pushed up, as usual, giving a bunched-up, blouson effect. His hair was still wet from his shower, so it looked darker, sleeker. His face was flushed.

'Well, no, it's not like inner-city Manchester,' he said.

'I wasn't comparing it to that.'

'I mean, if that's what you're used to, or if that's what you *like*, or if that's what you're *comfortable* with, I can see why you would hate it here. Of course.'

'I didn't say I hated it.'

'It's a quiet street. I moved here because it was quiet.'

'I know.'

'I moved here because I was sick of parties. I'd done nothing but go to parties for twenty fucking years. I didn't want that any more. If that's what *you* want, then you are in the wrong place, I'm afraid, honey.'

'Who mentioned parties? I was just saying...'

He smacked his hand onto the table then, hard.

'Why bring it up, then, *hm*? You're very fond of "just saying", aren't you? And then you expect me not to react.'

He stared at me for a couple of seconds, then picked up his cutlery, hunched over his plate. Outside, behind him, the wind carried the rain, the lamp posts quivered. I found myself thinking of certain people I knew – people not that far away – how surprised they'd be (wouldn't they?) to see me sitting there with that bright, bland expression on my face, trying to fence with this nonsense. Or had I been very naïve? Was this what life was like, really, and everyone knew it but me?

'You need to go back to Manchester, really, don't you?' Edwyn said, sympathetically.

I turned to him. He was smiling again. I joined him in that. I smiled.

'Well. No. And if you remember, I didn't come from Manchester. I was in Glasgow. Do you remember?'

'You need to go back to your friends in Manchester. This isn't for you, down here.'

'Where has this come from, Edwyn? Why are you being like this?'

'Being like what, honey?'

Not able to speak, I lifted my shoulders.

'Being like what?' he said. He was warmly interested now, leaning towards me.

'Just an, um…With an ugly tone?'

'A *what*, sorry?'

'An ugly tone. Telling me to go away. And I didn't say anything wrong. I didn't.'

'My tone is ugly? Hm. OK. Well. My tone *is* ugly, honey. Were you in the dark about that? Are you saying I deceived you about that? Are you saying I – what? – misled you in some way? I can assure you that I didn't. My tone *is ugly*. That's how I am. Because how I am, now, is I'm an *arsehole* and a fucking *cunt*. OK? I didn't used to be an *arsehole* and a fucking *cunt* but it's how I've ended up, OK?'

He stood up, took his plate, then put it down again, flexed his fingers.

'And isn't it just *too fucking sad*,' he said.

107

I didn't turn around, as he walked behind me, into the kitchen.
I kept looking out at the street. I heard Edwyn open the bin, tip in
what was left of his meal. Twice he tried to close the lid – slamming
it, which didn't work.

He came back, sat down, looked through me as he talked.

'You should know that I *am* sick,' he said. 'Just so long as you
know that. There's nothing nice about me. I don't have a nice bone
in my body. I know I can seem quite *comme il faut*, but that's not
me. OK?'

I don't think I had expected him not to react, as it goes. The expectation lagged a little, that's all. I was casting around for something
to say, and then as soon as I'd said it – 'lonely' – I knew what was
coming.

Finding out what you already know. Repeatingly. That's not sane,
is it? And while he might have said that this was *how he was*,
for me it continued to be frightening, panic-making, to hear the
low, pleading sounds I'd started making, whenever he was sharp
with me. This wasn't how I spoke. (Except it was.) This wasn't
me, this crawling, cautious creature. (Except it was.) I defaulted
to it very easily. And he let me. Why? I wonder now how much
he even noticed, hopped up as he was. No, I don't believe he
did notice. That was the lesson, I think. That none of this was
personal.

•

For table conversation back then, I'd got used to asking Edwyn questions, either about himself or about poets or painters or composers. He seemed to like that, I'd found, searching his memory, his mind, with narrowed eyes, a twitching mouth; scrunching and pleating his discerning bottom lip. I hadn't lived with anyone before. Never before had I sat down to eat with somebody every night. It was frightening. Daunting. Talking in triplicate, as Edwyn did, one question could last us all through a meal. He hedged everything with, 'As I'm sure you'll *know*,' which I didn't. I wanted to. That was nice of him, though, I thought, and I thought, He must be used to being the cleverest person in the room, which must be – again – lonely. Worse than lonely. I think he felt under siege. (Witness, for example, the little cache of weaponry in the hallway, in the dark wooden tub with the umbrellas: a hunting stick, an air rifle, a knobkerrie.)

So it was both strange, and dreadful – I knew it – to feel that I was managing him, in a way. Beyond bringing him out of himself, or my genuine interest; that I was maintaining this keen and appreciative front as a way to keep him calm, or to distract him. Like – I don't know – throwing some sausages at a guard dog. This was someone I was supposed to be close to. And wouldn't he be horrified if he knew that was how I saw it? His scorn would finish us both, I was sure. It was a deep instinct, though, as I was finding out. The deepest, in this new world? I had to hope not. But I was very much without bearings, that first year.

When I took my own plate out into the kitchen, Edwyn was

standing at the sink, gripping the edge of the surface, and breathing deeply.

'Do you want to skip tomorrow night?' I said. 'I don't mind.'

He turned around, smirked.

'No. We'll go. He's your friend, isn't he?'

'Yes, but. We don't have to. Or I could just go.'

'And you'll want to get drunk afterwards, will you?'

'No. Why do you have to say it like that?'

'Like what?'

'Oh, forget it. I'm sorry. It doesn't matter. Like nothing.'

'I have been to five thousand of these fucking events, OK?'

Now he slammed his hand against the side of the cupboard.

'I just want to know what I'm doing, OK?'

'OK. Well. I suppose I will want to have a drink. But I don't want to get drunk. I don't like getting drunk, really, these days.'

He looked at me with real hatred here. As if I were formidably evil. He stared at me, taking in what I'd said.

'I've been drunk once since you've known me. I don't think that's fair, Edwyn.'

'Yes. You drank until you were sick.'

'Right. OK. But we have been over that, haven't we? I've apologized so many times. I have, Edwyn.'

'And on my money. And all of your friends got drunk on my money. And you were sick. Nice.'

Whenever we had this conversation – every couple of weeks, it seemed, back then – I knew life was hopeless. I knew it was. My body started to ache. My voice got dull. I spoke like a machine that was running down, while he seemed only to gain energy.

'You offered to pay for the drink,' I said. 'I told you I'd pay you back when I could, and I will.'

He frowned.

'Don't be ridiculous. I don't want your money. And don't get me wrong, I was *happy* to pay, of course. You can't have a party with no wine.'

'I was happy not to have a party, if you remember.'

'Sure. But the fact is that you drank until you were sick. And your friends got drunk. On my money.'

'Right.'

There was a pause. Again I smiled, stupidly, pleadingly.

'Is that a *northern* thing, do you think?' he said.

'Is what a northern thing?'

'Well, you enjoy being sick on yourself, don't you? I've never known anyone else who enjoys being sick on themselves.'

'No.'

'So it's a reasonable question, then, isn't it? Is that what people in the north *do*? Is that something you find *acceptable*, or *civilized*, or *fun*? Perhaps it is. I wouldn't know.'

I didn't know how sick I'd been. Honestly. I was drunk. A dead weight. I could remember being yanked up stairs I couldn't climb.

'This is how you think it's going to be, do you?'

'This is what you think you're dragging me into, is it?'

I was lifted by the shoulders, thrown down with force. Lifted up, again.

'*You live in shit, so we all have to live in shit, is that right?*' Edwyn said.

Everything was rushing. His hatred. His changed face. I just kept trying to breathe.

'*Is it?*' he said, shaking me now. I said his name. Tried to. Was this it? Like drowning?

'Edwyn! Please!'

'*Don't you "Edwyn" me.*' He pulled me further into the flat, his hands under my armpits. '*You keep away from me.*'

I was lifted up again, by one arm, thrown down.

'*You keep well fucking away from me. OK? OK?*'

I stayed down, on the floor by the dresser, in the gap by the wall, on my hands and knees but not trying to stand, just ducking my head and keeping still.

'*Get back in the sewer,*' Edwyn said. '*Get back in the sewer, scum.*'

I opened my eyes to daylight. I was on the floor, in the store room. My eyes were watering. I felt I was surfacing, then sinking.

In painful stages I proceeded. In the bathroom I washed my face twice, cleaned my teeth twice. I sat down on the toilet seat to recover, moaning and crying with the pain. Finally I got down and knelt by the toilet, put my head down there. Cool, porcelain shoulder...

Edwyn's rucksack was still in the hallway. His coat was spread out on the bannister. So he hadn't gone to work. My handbag, I saw, had been emptied out onto the dresser. With shaking hands, I put everything back. Only my keys were gone. Did I remember that? Him taking them?

In the kitchen I cried while I ran the tap, and then I had to pause after every gulp of water, to suck in a breath, to squeeze my fists. There was Nurofen in the drawer, but when I shook the strip out of the box there were only two pills left, so I couldn't take them… I cried, again, painfully, when I saw that my suitcase was out, in the living room, open, and with all of my clothes thrown in, hangers and all. I remembered that too, now, Edwyn powering back and forth, while I stood like a ghost, just there, by the cooker.

Getting changed was painful. My body was like a puppet's body, my mind sloshing in my skull. I pulled off my sweaty dress, found some jeans, a jumper, then went to the bathroom again, and repeated my routine, brushing my teeth, my tongue, splashing cold water on my sore eyes, my flushed face. Then, again, I had to sit and wait out the room's violent fairground spinning.

What could help me? Who? The questions wrung me out. I pressed my teeth together and moaned.

Like a snake Edwyn rose from his slumber, his face flushed, crumpled, his blond hair hanging in pieces.

'What are you doing? What do you want?'

'Nothing. I just woke up in there. I wondered if you were awake.'

He stared at me.

'I don't remember much,' I said.

'Well. *Lucky you.*'

'Do you remember what happened? I'm sorry I got so drunk.'

Now he mimicked my voice:

'*What happened? What happened?* Don't you talk to me. Mad *bitch*. Mad *cunt*. *I* remember. *I* wasn't drunk.'

'*Don't you come near me,*' he said, as, stupidly, I stepped forward. '*What makes you think you can come near me?*'

The duvet was wrapped and ranged around his hips, his bare shoulders were pulled back: a bucking centaur.

I went back to the store room, heart pounding, teeth chattering. But what had I imagined? A hug? A 'never mind'? I couldn't think. I curled up in the club chair, waited.

Perhaps an hour passed before Edwyn appeared, dressed now, in his jeans, his huge flannel shirt, his cardigan. His eyes looked blasted.

'You're still here,' he said.

'Please, Edwyn. I'm so ill. I'm sorry. If I can just stay in here until I feel better. Then I'll go. I really don't think I can manage now.'

'I don't care how *you* feel. You think I care how *you* feel?'

'I know. I'm sorry. If I could just have an hour or two. I won't bother you.'

He was standing in the doorway, staring at me. Who'd liked me yesterday. Who'd let me come and live with him. I got down then, on my knees, and put my head down before him and said I was sorry over and over again.

'If I could just have a couple of hours' grace. Please, Edwyn.'

114

'Oh, you want a few hours' *grace* do you? *You* want a few hours' *grace*?'

I was looking at his bare feet. I edged back.

'Please. I feel so sick.'

Now there was a hand under my arm. A hand like a blade. I was yanked up.

'Well, if you feel sick, you better had move. Don't you dare be sick in here as well as every other room in the house.'

'I haven't been sick.'

'I've spent all night cleaning up your sick. You've been sick in every room in this flat.'

'Have I?'

'*Have I? Have I?*'

'I don't remember.'

'Oh, you think I'm making it up? You think I'm imagining it? *Christ*, I wish.'

He let me go and I walked to the bathroom. For a while I knelt and tried to be sick. Nothing. I sat with my mouth open, my heart-beat slamming in my head. Then I sat on the toilet seat. I took deep breaths, as if that would speed up the getting better. I kept twitching my feet, as if I could work it all off like that, somehow. I felt a heat flush through my body, and then a shivering cold.

Edwyn was waiting on the landing.

'You think I want to be a *carer*, do you? Is that what you think?' he said, as I tried to get past.

I shook my head.

'No.'

He followed me into the store room, where I sat down again, and curled up, put my hands over my head.

'Don't worry,' he said. 'I blame myself. I knew what I was getting. I knew what you *were*. You never learned, did you, how to interact with other people, in a way that wasn't mad. How to be in the world in a way that wasn't sick and mad...It's not your fault. I do understand that. But I won't be anyone's *carer*. Do you get that?'

'Oh, *you're* upset, are you? *You're* upset. Stop snivelling. Why do women snivel at everything?'

I was crying, but I didn't say anything any more. I was going to count to a hundred and then stand up. I was going to find my phone charger...Only I kept getting lost in my counting. My head throbbed. Self-disgust was an accelerant. Where could I go? There was nowhere. Nobody. I barely had tube fare. I was thirty-three and that was how it was. Backed into this same wretched corner. Worse each time, in fact. Trying to prove what, exactly?

Another hour passed. Another two hours.

To keep myself calm, I pictured a hotel room. In great detail. A kind place. Somewhere like the Kings Cross Inn. (Remember?) Where I could sleep and feel shaky tomorrow, fine on Thursday. In another world...By now I knew, I'd guessed, that Edwyn wasn't going to throw me out. But what came next in that case?

It started to get dark, cold. I heard the wind outside. And then

Edwyn appeared, again, in the doorway.

'There's nothing to eat,' he said.

'Oh.' I said. My mouth was so dry, it was hard to speak. 'Isn't there?' Again I had to swallow and wait. He stared at me.

'Do you want me to go and get something?'

'Well, I'm not going anywhere,' he said.

In the living room, while I laced up my boots, he came and walked around me. I was covered in sweat. A thick, cold, oily sweat.

'I won't buy meat,' I said.

'No one's asking you to buy meat. Did you hear me say that? Don't you put words into my mouth. I won't be told what I've said. *OK?*'

'You're just going to leave that there, are you?' he said, looking at my suitcase.

2

My grandmother was filthy. My father wasn't lying. And having had it pointed out by him, repeatingly, it grew hard to ignore: the greasy hair, the old make-up, drifting, in a varicoloured sludge. Long clouds of grime closed on her wrists and her throat, and there was that slightly rotten smell, too, abroad in her vicinity.

She did wash – herself, her clothes – but, inalienably mindful of the cost, she used cold water, and in the machine, just a snuff-pinch of soap and then a drop of TCP. So – wash isn't the word, is it? She conscientiously got herself and her clothes wet; the effectiveness of this enterprise: not relevant, somehow. Not what she was being marked on.

We lived with her after my mother left my father, for four years, until I was eight. During that time she was observant about my being clean, in one respect: she insisted on checking me over after I'd been to the toilet. I had to bend over and touch my toes while she went at me with her crispy, barely damp flannel – a mould-bloomed rag – rubbed repeatedly on one of the cracked old bars of soap she collected. These sat banked around the taps. Black in the cracks. Cracked like bark.

But was anybody clean back then? When I think of my friends' houses, they weren't any less filled with shit. Here were cold, cluttered bedrooms, greased sheets. The kitchens were a horror show: ceilings bejewelled with pus-coloured animal fat, washing-up sitting in water which was spangled like phlegm. Our neighbour's house, where we went after school, was an airlocked chamber smelling of bins that hadn't been put out. There was a long skid mark, I remember, on one of the towels in their bathroom. It was there for three years.

So – I did grow up in shit. It was no slander.

Shit, filth, stupidity, dishonesty. (Mother looking up slyly from a crying jag.)

I did use to be sick a lot. *No slander*, though Edwyn didn't know it. I don't think he ever asked about my past, my old lives, which was either sensitivity, discretion or – I don't know – does it show that his idea of me was fragile? I think I was sick from drink, at least once a week, for about fifteen years. In Manchester, everything made me sick. I was lonely, frightened. I couldn't manage. I look back on a decade of barely managed helplessness. I'd wake up to people I didn't know, looking at my things. One tall, bald man in a leather jacket:

'So are you quite a lonely character? Me too. So do you really not get out much? Me neither. I bet you don't read biographies, do you? No, I *do*. Now come here, you. Come on.'

Once I woke up in a hotel in town, to a long heap of sick next to me in bed, like a person.

And the men I thought interesting, liked – I only ever woke up with them through some drunken accident, usually because they were at a low in their lives. I remember coming round with my old friend Kerrigan, from home, whom I adored:

'I'm just wondering why you want to *annihilate* everything,' he was saying, looking round my flat for his clothes. I didn't remember what I'd done.

Time doesn't help. You forget, for years, even, but it's still there. A zone of feeling. A cold shade. I barely drink now, but when I do, sometimes I see so clearly how nothing's changed. Not one thing. About who I am and what I am. I don't have to be drunk. When I least expect it, my instincts are squalid, my reactions are squalid, vengeful. And for what? What am I so outraged by? Little mite with a basilisk stare. Grown woman. My parents were hopeless. And? Helpless, as we all are. Life *is* appalling. My father ate himself to death. Isn't that enough? A year before that, in a short email to my brother, he mused,

> 'Should I tell you/shield you? The latest. Peri-anal
> abscesses! Pain unimaginable!'

Won't that do?

•

Kerrigan lives down here now, sharing a flat in a block in Kent-ish Town. I went and met him for a coffee, earlier this year. His suggestion. A happy surprise, when my phone buzzed. I walked up to Café Rustique one warm and rainy afternoon, after work.

My old friend stood up as I opened the door, and edged out deftly from his side of the table to give me a hug.

'Are you wet or are you shiny?' he said, pausing. (I had on my black plastic mac.)

'Hello. Yeah, I'm both. Do you want to risk it?'

'I do. What d'you want? D'you want a coffee? No, I'll get it, you sit down, darling.'

Christ, he looked thin. Thin little legs. People do get old, when you look away. I looked old. Hair in a frizz. When he sat back down, he smiled again. His cheeks were raked under his whiskers, as if by rain. I liked his new glasses, though.

'They're good,' I said.

'Oh, thanks. Yeah.'

He took them off and looked at them, gave them a polish with his cardigan sleeve, pushed them back on again.

I felt we were in some other stream of life, somehow. We'd known each other for so long, and then we hadn't. He told me about his work, in Wormwood Scrubs, now, the woman he'd been seeing, how he was trying to get a more permanent job.

'It's dead-men's shoes these days,' he said. 'More or less.'

He had a flatmate who worked in a phone shop. He was always avoiding him.

'It's like being at school again, you know, hiding in the toilet for a bit of privacy? I've had to clear out today while his kid comes round and you do find yourself thinking, nothing's changed, when you're still, you know, killing time in places like this. I was brushing my teeth in there before,' he said, nodding at the gents'.

We caught up on the people we knew: Margaret, Paul Powell. I told him about my father's funeral. I knew he had family in that neighbourhood, too.

'Oh, yeah, I know the place,' he said. 'I think they planted my old man there. *Think* so.'

'When was that?'

'Oh, God, years ago. Five years?'

'Did you go?'

'No. No, I don't go back any more. Feel a bit afraid to, if I'm honest. Has a radioactive feel now. Like it would be hazardous! Not reaching the full Chernobyl levels yet. But getting there, you know?'

'I feel that for Manchester more than Liverpool. But yes. Strange, isn't it? Blameless places. But not.'

'No,' he said, and he squinted at his drink, then looked back up at me with his eyes still narrowed.

'What do you get up to down here?' I said.

'Oh. Well. Lots of this, to be honest. Lots of coffee. Coffee with the clients. Coffee with my boss. You know I don't drink now? Well, *now* you know. Coffee in the evening. I'm working, mostly. Getting about. I never know where I'm going to be, so. *Gadding. Jaunting.*'

My coffee was too strong. I dragged a teaspoon through it and watched it lap at the sides of its silly French bowl. While Kerrigan went to get himself a refill, I looked around the café, which was quite busy: lots of young faces in computer light, one fattish man in a body warmer, absently feeding bits of flapjack to his dog. When Kerrigan came back, we both tuned in for a while to the woman next to us, an Irish woman, with a dainty face, and her maroon hair *en brosse*. She was on her phone, and stirring her tea, then flicking through a magazine.

'No, but she's OK in Beaverbrooks, isn't she? Ah…She's so good with people. Well, she can't compare…I said to her, life's different now, you can't compare like that. She has to put it behind her, that old life. Ah, did you? Well, you're very grown up these days. What are you like? No, I can't thank everybody enough. I had a very special afternoon. I was a bit heavy-hearted, but I do have such lovely memories. So I'm just going to look out of the window now and chill. And think about everybody and how lovely it all was. Now if you go into Timpsons, will you say hello to the lads there for me? Will you?'

Outside the sunset abetted one last queer revival of light, so the outlook was torched; wet bus stop, wet shutters, all deep-dyed.

Kerrigan and I said goodbye at the station.

I waited for the lift, and shivered.

3

When I first came down, to visit, this struck me as a real old-style bachelor's room. Shipshape. Unfussy. I did my hair in a small, poxed mirror, hung up on a nail. On the chest of drawers was Edwyn's tortoiseshell comb, his cologne bottle, the glass ashtray where he put his watch at night. At least it's cooler in here, in the summer. The sunlight comes filtered through ragged summer greenery. Fuzzy shadows move on the blue-grey walls.

Edwyn emptied half of his wardrobe for me when I moved in, and I started to take care of my clothes, too, hanging them up as he did, lining my shoes up next to his. He also bought a new bed, and over the course of those first few months had the hallway and the living room repainted.

'Well, it's a new start, isn't it?' he said. 'I've been meaning to do all this and now I've got a reason to.'

The day I moved in, I arrived at Euston in the early evening, stepping off the train with a holdall to shoulder, somehow, over my winter cape, and a suitcase to drag on its one working wheel. Edwyn hurried down the ramp to meet me: overcoat, long stride. He gave me a hard hug, his hat in his hand.

That was January. Each day brought just a few hours of dampened light, and the few friendships I'd thought to broach down here fell into desuetude, as I didn't go out, didn't answer emails, then felt guilty and answered carelessly, at too great a length. I didn't want to see anyone, really, apart from Edwyn, as deep into April the temperature remained jammed at freezing. I got wrapped up and walked out with him every morning, up to Earl's Court, then took the tenner he gave me to the supermarket and bought something for our tea. Just vegetables, I mean; pulses, seeds, nuts for protein. I learned to cook, quite well, having never bothered with a recipe before. Four floors up, lying on the new bed, I'd look up from my work and cherish the peace. I'd start making dinner at seven, and by eight I'd be at the window, watching for Edwyn.

Then I was sick, that night, after my party.

Then in September I got my job.

My father died in January. We got married in June. When we got back here that day we lay on the bed with the fan on, dozed a little and held each other. Edwyn told me things about himself that he said no one else knew and I felt close to him.

When this was a family house, this floor was for the children. This would have been the nursery, or half of it. Now the chest of drawers fills one narrow alcove, and a bookcase with locked glass doors stands in the other.

I see Edwyn sitting on the end of the bed, thoughtful, happy, a pile of those art books next to him.

I see him sleeping on his back. Fine, lank blond hair, weathered skin. Both hands on the pillow, in loose fists.

My problem finds a symbol, I think, in my insisting, for so long, on trying to kiss him on the mouth. I knew he didn't like it. Yet if we were sitting together, or lying together, I would keep leaning in. At which he'd turn his face, lift his chin. More than that: he'd tighten his grip and steer me away. I didn't get that message. I chose instead a mounting fretfulness. Saying goodbye in the morning, at the station, I continued to stand there after our hug, eyes closed, head tilted up, only to find he'd walked off.

Once when I tried in bed, he sat up and leant away from me.

'Don't you get it?' he said. 'I want to do things when I want to do them.'

'But you never do,' I said (I whined). 'Why can't I say anything about that? It's just a kiss.'

'Christ, will you listen to yourself? How do I get out of this? *How?*'

He got out of bed then, with a jerk, and then, I don't know, he must have just roamed the flat for a bit. Working off his anger, I thought. But no. When he came back, I could tell it wasn't over. We lay there side by side for a while, and I kept hearing him take a breath, as if he were about to speak. Dissolved in the dark, the pressure this built up was horrible. I felt my jaw clenching, my heart going.

'Can I ask you a question?' he said, finally.

'OK.'

'What makes you think you can treat me like this, hm? When *I'm* making the money, *I'm* paying the bills, *I'm* making your life possible.'

I didn't answer. I didn't know.

'What part of my being ill don't you understand?' Edwyn said. 'What part of "no" don't you understand? *Hm?* I am *in pain*, all of the time. OK?'

My eyes started to sting. But now his tone changed, as it often did. Now he spoke in his soft voice, his understanding voice.

'You can't *help* it,' he said. 'I know you can't. Women *are* sex-obsessed. I know it's all they think about. It's all they give a fuck about, really.'

Still I didn't stop. I insisted on a different picture: him peering out meanly from the crenels. Little boy in a tablecloth cape, in a sandcastle fort, seeing how hugely his terrible shadow falls. And if I could just talk him down…

There is something dreadful in that. Something frightening, when he was so ill, worn out. In my suggesting 'other things'. What did I expect? And wasn't it humiliating, trying to put that into words, with him narrowing his eyes at me? He said he couldn't see the point. *Didn't I get it?* he said. 'That's not sex, for me, there's

128

nothing enjoyable about it. It's supposed to be a preamble, it's pointless on its own.'

And besides, sex for him had to be spontaneous, he had to feel overwhelmed, overcome. If it was planned out, he felt *nothing*. Later he decided he'd 'always hated sex'. 'It's just one more thing women *want* from you,' he said.

By then any physical hint made him furious. And well it might. I wasn't listening, was I?

'What's the matter now? I've got to go to *work*. You don't *get* that, do you?'

'Christ, you stink. Your breath stinks. You smell like rotten vegetables.'

I tried being silly. Holding on to his shoulder in the morning, wiggling about.

'What are you doing?'

'I'm being saucy.'

'That's saucy, is it? Who told you that was attractive? Seriously. Where did you get the idea that *that* was sexy? In any way.'

'I wasn't trying to be sexy. I was just being silly.'

'No, I'm serious. That's what you think is sexy, is it? That's what passes for sexy in your world, does it? Why would you think that was attractive? What is it about that that you think *anyone* would find appealing?'

For days after that first row, when I was sick, I mean, Edwyn didn't like to touch me at all. He was uncomfortable when I hugged him.

When I reached my arms out he looked at me as if he knew exactly what I was composed of, was marvelling at my malignancy, that nature could endorse such a contrivance. Still, we continued to sit down together for dinner. I tried to get through it. One night, feeling the silence, I said I must like to be cast out, mustn't I?

'Sure,' Edwyn said. 'Looks like it. But that's not my problem. I hope you see that. I'm not *interested* in that.'

If I could just have taken that in. Then, and later. It took me a long time, months, of plays and niggles. Hopeful looks. As birds drum on the earth to bring up the worms, I suppose, until I got what I really wanted, which turned out to be – a different kind of fulfilment:

'Love for you is *possession*, isn't it?' Edwyn said, abruptly, one evening as we finished another quiet meal. The end of a long train of thought, evidently.

'Is it?' I said. 'I don't know. Go on.'

'It's jealous and mean. It's smothering…Like a *swamp*. You're like a baby, really, aren't you? You won't be happy until we're both just crawling around this place in our own *shit*.'

That rang truer. I felt a dullness seep into my system: the feeling of having been found out. I had thought in the past, wondered, trying to be close to people, if there wasn't something about me that might horrify them. What might they see?

Edwyn went on:

'Of course I should have seen it coming. I blame myself, don't worry. Everything turns to shit. Put two people together and it turns to shit almost instantly. I should have explained that, when you wanted to move in. I should have said, if you don't want this to turn to *shit*, then stay away. But you were sweet, and you seemed to want it so badly...'

Was it my idea? I couldn't remember. (Another lacuna. I should keep track of them, shouldn't I? It isn't good enough, to keep blanking on these points. Not to have shaken myself free of it, this fog.)

'Didn't you want it?' I said.

'No. It was you. Don't start changing the facts. I'm not trading in fantasy here. You wanted to move in. I didn't want it. I never wanted to live with anybody. There is a reason why I've spent my life alone. This is the reason. Because women are insane, and manipulative, and sick. But you were very clear on what was going to happen. And I was stupid, I'll admit that, I'll take full responsibility for that: I let you have your way.'

'Right. I see. OK.'

'I keep asking myself what it *was* about you that made me do this, made me get into it, up to my neck...I think I thought, She's a writer, she'll understand that we don't own each other. But your world is very you-centred, isn't it? Very infantile. Do you think the world, for me, should start and end with *you*? Perhaps you do...Is that it?'

'No, of course not.'

'What do I do to get out of this? Do I kill myself? Don't think I don't think about it. Don't think that doesn't go round and round in my head all day, every day. Don't think I don't know that's what you want, too. I can see it. I can see the *resentment*, and the *rage* boiling over...'

'I'm not resentful. I'm grateful.'

'I've got my heart disease trying to kill me, I've got this *condition*, so I'm always in pain, and I've got *you*. I'm paying for something... Well, that's it, from now on. I'll do what I like, you do what you like. You don't have to worry about any of this any more.'

'Worry about what?'

'This. Cooking. Eating together. You hate it. I'm sick of having to rush because you finish in five minutes and then sit there filled with fury. At having to sit with me, spend any time with me, spend any time doing anything which isn't exactly what you want to do.'

'I don't mind cooking. I'm not furious. I like trying to make healthy things.'

'No, you're done with it. By the time you've prepared a meal you're boiling over with anger and resentment, I can feel it. I feel it when you sit down. That's it for you. Enough time wasted on me. You've said yourself that you'd just take a pill if you could. You don't like food. You don't like meals. Eating together, enjoying somebody's company like an adult, it's not for you, is it? That's fine, I understand. Children get bored at the table. I used to resent every second sitting with the grown ups. I don't want either of us to force each other to be what we're not. You hate having to sit here with me, whereas for me, after a day at work, having my supper is something I look forward to. It's not the same for you, of course. You're here all day. But do you see? This is one of the few fucking pleasures left in my life. And now I'm in the last few years of my *fucking* miserable life. *OK?* And I don't want *this*, anymore.'

'Please don't be so vicious.'

'I'm not being vicious. I'm not being vicious, honey, I'm stating a few facts, here. You're supposed to like facts, aren't you?'

'You called me a child.'

'When did I call you a child? You hear what you want to hear, don't you? I said children get bored at the table, which they do. I know what I said. I won't have my words, twisted, *OK*? I've had enough of that. I won't live in your fantasy world. You won't drag me into the *shit pit* where you live, *OK*? I don't know if you're confusing me with your *father*, but I'm not joining in with that, *OK*?'

I took my things into the kitchen, then came back out and sat on the settee. I thought the row was over. I was thinking about what he'd said. But he stood up and kept talking, as he took his own stuff out to the sink:

'I'm a carer, aren't I? That's what I've become. You need constant attention. You can't be left alone. You can't be an adult, I don't know why…But *again*, it is my own fault. I knew what I was getting. I knew you were damaged.'

Here I had to tell him that I had always lived alone. That attention was not something I craved, partly – since he'd brought him up – because I'd hated my father's interest so much. Strange what one gets pedantic about, but there you are…What else was I going to dispute?

'You mean you were on benefits,' Edwyn said.

'I was on tax credits, but that's not what I'm talking about. I'm saying I have no problem being alone. I've always been independent. That's all.'

'Oh, independent. Ah. OK. Funny definition you have of that word.'

'No, it's not. I don't need constant attention. That's all I'm saying. I do try and kiss you, that's true, but I can stop. I will, don't worry.'

'As I say, whatever cosy spin you want to put on it. But don't say you were independent. You were living off the state. You were on benefits.'

'Why are we talking about this? You get tax credits when you are employed. I was doing fine. But that's not the point I was making.'

'Well, I'm not as up on all of that as you are. But where I'm from, being independent means being able to look after yourself. That's what that word means, do you understand? I know I'm more or less alone in giving a fuck what words mean any more. Independent. It's just a brain-dead feminist flag to fly for women who haven't got a man. Your generation has a funny attitude.'

'You don't listen to me.'

'*Listen* to yourself…Christ, *listen* to yourself, honey. You sound like a twelve-year-old. A twelve-year-old trying to win an argument. This isn't an argument. You don't *get* that, do you?'

4

A 'childish sense of drag', did I say? To feel 'shut down inside'. But certain impulses do persist. I found myself visiting my mother this April; leaving the house one morning and heading to Euston instead of to the supermarket. This was the first time I'd seen her since Glasgow.

'Oh, you'll be so proud of me,' she said. 'I've been going to Oxfam every day. I'm surprised they haven't started turning me away! I just kept thinking, Will I ever use this again? *No.* So – yes, I'm embracing minimalism!'

This observance was not immediately in evidence in the 'bachelorette pad'. She'd been there for more than a year by then, but seemed still to be only half moved in. There were two old, broken Hoovers in the hallway, and a row of grey Stack 'n' Store baskets, narrowing the way, and a bin bag full of toiletries by the bathroom door.

'Now they're on my list,' she said, 'to sort out. Oh, but *do* go through it all and see if you want anything. It's mostly little bottles from hotels. Body lotion, shower gel. Endless little soaps.'

She'd bought a ground-floor flat in a modern block behind Oxford Road. The New Foundry. It was a nice place, cosy-feeling, as those conversions often aren't. She even had a small balcony, or terrace, maybe: it was just a few feet off the ground, looking out on a bit of undeveloped ex-car park, bounded by the railway bridge.

'Yes, so that's my *outside space*,' she said. '*Now*. Do you want to give me your coat, Neve? And do you want a cup of tea?'

'OK. Yes, please.'

There was something haphazard about her arrangements. The living room and kitchen were open plan, but she'd bought what she told me now was 'a *room divider*': in fact an overbearing black bookcase, which served to make both areas feel cramped.

'Don't you keep walking into it?' I said. 'You maniac. Isn't the whole point that they aren't divided?'

'*Mm...*' she said. She was filling the kettle.

I went out onto the terrace and soon enough she joined me.

'Now, that's all my bulbs, should be coming up soon,' she said, pointing at one tub. 'And that's my little bird-feeding buffet there...'

'That's elaborate.'

'I know, yes, well, I get all sorts there, now. Tits and robins and blackbirds and a *jay*, one morning. There's a goose waddles round from the canal. Lots of LBJs.'

'What's that?'

'That is a bird-watching term! Little brown jobbies! There's a pigeon who comes but he's so stupid he just sits in the water dish!'

'And are they your nosey neighbours?' I said, nodding up at two men sitting squashed together on their steel balcony, in a redbrick block on the other side of the waste ground.

'Oh, yes, the gay couple, yes, that's them, they're always out, all weathers. There's an old one and a young one. The old one sits out and drinks in the afternoon. The young one just appears in the mornings in his onesie, having a cigarette. He came up to me in the Spar the other day. I thought, Oh, no, he's going to tell me they can see me getting undressed! But he didn't. He said, "Excuse me? You live in the flat opposite ours, don't you?" So I said, "Er, *yes*?" And he said, "Did you know there's a tramp sleeps under your balcony every night?" So – I just sort of shrugged, really. What does he want me to do about it?'

'I don't know. I suppose some people wouldn't like it, would they?'

'I don't care what people do. What's it to me? I just said, "OK."' She frowned.

'He probably just enjoyed telling you.'

'Well – I don't know.'

'Did I just hear the kettle turn off?'

'Oh. Yes. Sorry.'

She edged past me to get back inside and I followed her in and slid shut the door behind me. It was cold out there.

I'd been distracted, too, while we were talking, by her right eyelid, which was drooping. Only a mean little chink of that eye was visible.

'Is there something wrong with your eye?'

'Is there? Which one? What do you mean?'

'Your right eye. It's half shut. Is it sore?'

'Ooh, is it? Wait there. Just. Oh. I can't do two things. Can you get this tea, Neve? Now where's my bag? Does it look bad, Neve?'

I took our tea around-about the 'room divider' and over to the settee.

'It's noticeable. It looks like when you don't pull the blinds up properly.'

She came back with her lipstick mirror, peering at herself.

'Oh dear. Well. What blind's that? I can't see!'

She turned the light on and came and sat down next to me, still grinning into the mirror.

'*Now*,' she said. 'Of course I did have the first of my *cataract* operations last week, so I suppose it could be that. That's supposed to wear off, though!'

'Do they just do one eye at a time?'

'Mm...Yes, in case it goes wrong, I suppose. Oh, I hope it wears off!'

She tilted her head further back, into the light. She touched her eyelid, and bared her teeth at the tiny mirror.

My mother was growing her hair by then. It lay in chancy locks around her neck, held back from her face that day by a padded Alice band.

'Is that new?' I said. 'That hairband.'

'Oh. This? Yes, it is. What do you think?'

She put the mirror down then, and turned from side to side, showing off her 'do. The band was made of sparkly black velvet. It looked like something girls used to wear when I was in infant school. Or posh girls in sitcoms. Sarah Ferguson, did she have one? That kind of person.

'I'm not sure,' I said.

'Oh. Well, I saw someone wearing something similar and I thought I'd try it. While I'm at this *intermediate stage*. It's only from Poundland. Now, is that tea OK?'

'Yes. I made it, remember.'

'Oh, yes, of course you did.'

What she most wanted to do that afternoon was to show me her photos, from an unlikely trip she'd made to California, to stay with Eric. He was a visiting professor at USC by then. I don't know how she finagled the invite, but off she'd gone, to spend a week in Los Feliz, in the apartment the university had provided him with.

Her pictures – she clicked through them on her computer while I stood at her shoulder – were mostly of the apartment: long strips of windows (ragged palm trees behind), a wall of glass bricks, a breakfast bar, a fire pit.

'Yes, it was very *Modernist*,' she said. One lampshade in particular, evidently. She'd taken half a dozen pictures of it.

'Another one of the lampshade, ha ha! Yes, that was *very* Modernist, Eric said.'

'Did you leave the house?'

'I *did*. But not as much as I'd have liked, no. I didn't have a car,

139

obviously, so it's not easy to get around. It's hot buses everywhere, so…Wouldn't you think if you had a guest you might, you know, maybe take her out for dinner one night? A meal by the ocean? Offer to show her around Los *Angeles*, or the campus? Well, he didn't. He took me to a diner for a sandwich on my last day there, but I had to force him into that. And it was horrible. Disgusting. "Canadian Ham", which is Spam, basically.'

I didn't stay the night. I met Margaret for a drink and then took a late train home.

The flat was dark when I arrived. The bedroom, too, so I stayed out in the hallway to get undressed. To no avail, as it turned out. As I got into bed, the light came on. Edwyn sat up, frowned.

'Oh, hello. You're awake.'

'I am now.'

'Oh dear. Sorry. Were you really asleep?'

'I was trying to fall asleep.'

Here he blinked and shook his head.

'How are your poor poorly paws?' I said.

'Oh. Yes. Tender.'

'*Tender!* Oh, no. Let's see.'

I sat up, and he lifted a hand and I held it. He looked at me trustingly.

'Naughty paw,' I said, and I stroked his hand and then his other hand, an equal number of times. I put my face on his hand.

'I love you.'

'I love *you*,' he said. 'Did you have a nice visit?'

'Yes, it was all right. Same old thing.'

I lay back down, and faced him on the pillow. He looked drawn, worn out. I told him about my mother's flat.

'Mm…Well, old ladies do just stop bothering, I'm afraid,' he said. 'No husband any more, no kids, they just decide to live in filth. Stop cleaning the house, stop keeping themselves clean, or feeding themselves properly. My mother was the same. She'd just eat white bread and jam, unless I went round and cooked for her. So she held that over me. And she started drinking, of course. She could get out to go to the pub all right, with her mad neighbour. Christ, I hated him. Always appearing over the fence. I mean, she made me hate her, really. She made me despise her. Isn't that dreadful? What did she want, really? A bit of attention.'

'I didn't say it was filthy. Well, you might think it was.'

'No. Well. I don't know what to say, then. What was your point?'

'No point. Nothing, really. She doesn't want much, either. On the face of it, anyway. A friend or two. She must have spent a fortune on that trip, just to sit there. I wonder what this Eric thinks is going on?'

'He probably just thinks she's a mad old lady.'

'Right.'

'Can you turn the light off?'

'Yes, sorry. Let's go to sleep.'

'My hands hurt.'

'OK.'

We lay in the dark for a while. Then he stroked my back a bit, my shoulders, with his curled up hand.

'I love you. Little one. Little Neve. I do.'

I could have been asleep. I let some peaceful seconds pass, before I said it back.

'I love *you*.'

5

After that French sojourn, I touched down in Glasgow on a Friday evening, walked from the station to the underground with my holdall bouncing on my back. The air was fumy. The smell of chips came in thin, damp draughts from the arches. Here were greasy, littered streets; a warm, rainy, dark-blue dusk.

At home I went straight to bed. I pulled the yellow fleece blanket from the cupboard's top shelf and cosied up against the cold. I'd got into the habit of listening to late-night radio, while I lived there. The phone-ins. I clicked on the set then, before I turned off the light, as outside the gutter dripped sloppily, fitfully:

'But when the monsters come, listen, Stu, I nearly killed my dog last time. I just. I'm telling you. I've got a seven-foot garden, I never go in it, I keep my curtains closed.'

My curtains were drawn. I liked the night sky, cool air, crowding chimney pots.

'And er…that saved her you see, Stu, I was going to kill her it was all I'd been thinking about but then that saved her that she said that Oh, would you like a cup of tea? Because I'd been ready that was what I was thinking of when I went round there and when I knocked on the door. So I think that does go to show really that if only women could be less antagonistic and we could all just talk and as I say, have a cup of tea…'

When I got back from the supermarket, the next day, Kit-Kat was on my couch, stretched out in a milky sunspot. I sat with her while my first lot of washing went through. I avoided my bed, which was covered in bills that needed dealing with.

Money was about to be a problem. In an attempt to see that off, I headed out again, to the café under Stevie's place. It was a nice, chilly day: last night's rain still slathering the pavement. I took a coffee to a computer and scrolled through Gumtree, answered half a dozen ads – cafés, shops. Reading the applications back, as I waited out my slot, I detected an unbalanced enthusiasm. Would anyone notice? I wrote another handful of replies, more carefully this time, and then called Stevie, with a 'Guess who?' He was in, doing nothing. I still had some fellowship cash, so I said I'd take him out. We stayed out, too, even though he kept saying he had to be up in the morning.

By three a.m., sitting on the floor in his hallway, he was saying, 'Spit in my mouth! Go on!'

I scrunched up one eye to aim. Then, 'Now you!' he said. 'Open up!'

His son lived in Kilcreggan with his parents. We drove up there, in the morning. I walked on the beach while he made his visit, my footsteps slurring through the shale.

After Edwyn and I were married I tried to plot a new path. I cleared out the store room – a bit – put the club chair back in the living room. I bought a small desk, which I have against the wall, under the skylight.

In a new notebook, I wrote down his line: *'It's freedom that counts.'* Did I believe it? It didn't seem to be what I'd aimed for. The opposite, rather. An illusion of freedom: snap-twist getaways with no plans: nothing real. I'd given my freedom away. Time and again. As if I had contempt for it. Or was it hopelessness I felt, that I was so negligent? Or did it hardly matter, in fact? If I could just dissolve myself, as I always had, in time, in art, when I felt loss or lack. I learned about that when I was little. The other world. That's what I had to guard, wasn't it?

I wrote down, things like:

Untangle yourself. Stop saying you love him. You're wearing a groove in your mind. Say it when you mean it. Save money. Small steps. Save money every month. Remember you're a grown woman now. Be more proud and more relaxed. Don't feel persecuted by stupid students. Don't think about them. Don't

*let your mind get colonized. Get on with your work. Don't pet
him. Don't act like a baby. Don't be a cat. Be decent to him and
to yourself. Respect yourself and him. See your friends. Don't be
sly. Don't be deceitful. Don't snoop. Don't ask him questions for
the sake of it, it's lonely-making to sit and listen when he's said
it before, when he won't let you in. Keep your footing. Leave the
room if he calls you a name. If you save money you can leave
the flat if he's nasty. Stand up for yourself but don't waste your
energy. This is your time and your energy. Don't try and 'manage'
him. Be natural and let him be natural. That's what love is. No
more cramped feelings, on either side.*

How did these small steps fare? Strangely. Keeping myself to
myself more. Sometimes it felt like we'd done it. Sometimes not.
Sometimes he whimpered in pain and I was Mrs Pusskins again,
and what was wrong with that? It felt soothing. Coming home
from work, standing on the landing, he'd open his mouth and lift
his arms for a hug, and we'd hold each other and I'd feel safe and
happy, with someone I could love in a natural way.

Once, when I was in the living room after he'd gone to bed, he
came in and did a little pirouette in his Y-fronts, trying to get me to
look. I did look up and smile, but I didn't run to him, like I used to,
didn't fuss him. Was that wrong? He performed a hurt little moue
in the proscenium, before walking off slowly with an 'I say' and a
sort of half-toddlerish wobbling walk.

'That was a good dance!' I called after him, stupidly.

I did see my friends more, stayed later at work to do my own work.

One night I told him how things were panning out with my father's estate. There was a buyer, at last, for the house, and once his debts were cleared there was going to be about £25,000 left, to be split between me and my brother. There was a lot of debt: credit cards and a bankruptcy, secured against the house. Then there was what we owed Patrick for making the place saleable (my father hadn't done any upkeep, in twenty-five years.)

'I suppose you'll want to leave me now,' Edwyn said.

'Don't be silly.'

'Well. I've been thinking we need to get your bookcases built, don't we? I must ring Warren and get the number for his man, see if he's got time to do that this month. It's ridiculous you not having your things here, but I never had a moment, and I was ill…'

'I know. That's OK. Thank you. That'll be brilliant, to have my books.'

I was very moved by that, in that it seemed to mean he did want me around, and I fussed him as I'd told myself not to, and he seemed happy.

Only the next day, it went wrong again. As he came in with some shopping, I was telling him about my afternoon. I had a friend who'd started a new job, and she'd been amusing about it and I was just trying to recreate that, I suppose, her little pen portraits. She worked for a children's charity and the office was decorated with child-safety posters, each featuring a cartoon of a potential threat.

147

A toddler investigating a hanging blind cord. A child reaching for a butcher's knife. I was trying to describe this, not very well, I expect, but I chattered on.

Edwyn passed me something and I continued to talk, looking at what was in my hand too late.

'"Thank you for my walnuts."'

'Sorry?'

'I've bought you some walnuts. You don't think you should say thank you?'

'I was in the middle of telling you something. I didn't notice. Edwyn? Thank you. Of course.'

'You think I just exist to sort of cater to you, is that it?'

'Edwyn. I say thank you every day for what you do for me. I say thank you after every meal, what's going on?'

He walked out then, left the bags, put his rucksack back on.

'I'll go to the pub, I don't want to sit with a defensive whiner. Do you want me to eat out more? Is this all too much trouble for you?'

'What are you talking about? Don't go out, please. I just didn't notice what you'd handed me.'

His shoulders were rounded and he was looking at me fearfully, as if I were a threat.

It was no choice but an instinct, I was sure, a law of his being, this ripping the ground away. So I couldn't quibble. I had to accept it or not. And after all it couldn't be very nice for him. So with warm energy, I sought to reassure him, and thank him, and tell him what was coming for tea. He let himself be coaxed, eventually.

The tension could make me sick, leading up to our worst rows. I remember getting cramps from hearing the bathroom light turned on and off. Click-ping! Click-ping! A pause. Click-ping! He was going to test it until it broke.

'Fuck!' he shouted, when it did. And then I heard him kick the door.

That night with the walnuts, I knew things weren't settled, and sure enough, after tea, something on the TV set him off. We were watching a silly crime show, as we often did. In this one the pretty village school teacher was confiding to her friend over coffee and bickies:

'Clive's just not the man I married,' she said. She was a gamine little thing, with hennaed hair, and draped in scarves, as arty types are in these productions.

Edwyn said,

'Disappointed *cunt*. Resentful *bitch*.'

'What's that?'

'Men get older, and their cunt wives are "disappointed" and they're treated like dirt. Evil shallow fucking bitches. Oh, *he isn't the man I married*. Stupid shallow cunt. Disappointed cunt, drinking in disappointment with the air you fucking breathe.'

I should have just gone to bed then, that's what I'd told myself to do.

'When did women become so resentful?' Edwyn went on. 'They didn't use to be resentful, they used to be happy with a home, children...'

'Did they? That's a new one.'

'For generations, they were happy with a home, a husband and children. That's all they wanted.'

'No, it's not.'

'In the past they were happy with a home, a husband…'

'I heard you the first time. If they were so happy…'

'They were happy with a home, a husband…'

'You've said this four times, why do you keep repeating it? You're frightening me.'

'They were happy with a home, a husband and children. This silly feminist shit, it's beneath you. Women were happy.'

'Edwyn, are you in there? What are you doing?'

His expression – chin up, staring straight ahead – was complacent, haughty. And then it changed, as if an acid had burnt off that layer.

'If you ever let me finish a fucking sentence, then I wouldn't need to repeat myself, would I?' he said, rounding on me.

'You did finish it. You did finish it, then you kept on saying it! *Edwyn, please…*'

'Christ. This is what I've got to look forward to, is it? *Jesus…* This fishwife, whining voice… You know, I'm convinced half of this pain is psychosomatic, and I'm looking at the cause. Cunt.'

I got up and went to the bathroom then, washed my face, brushed my teeth. I had learnt, after all. That once it had happened, I should say as little as possible. There never was any way to dismantle what they said. There just wasn't. I went to bed. For a while I could hear him bashing about in the kitchen. Later, when he came in, he turned on the big light, tried to slam the door (it doesn't really slam), and got undressed angrily.

In the morning, he didn't get up when his alarm went off. Instead he just kept sighing loudly.

'What's the matter?' I said.

He didn't answer, just turned his head slightly away. Was he going to just lie there?

'Are you not talking to me?' I said.

After a while he said,

'Nongsematter.'

'Is it your angiogram? That's today, isn't it?'

Again, after a long while, after I'd asked him again, he deigned to shrug.

'OK,' I said, and I turned over, reached for my phone to look at my emails.

'I don't know.'

'You don't know what?'

'I don't know if it's that.'

'Right.'

I didn't ask for details. I didn't say sorry, as I used to, whether I felt I'd done anything wrong or not. He never apologized. If I pressed him to, after he'd called me a name, for instance, or broken something, it only ever made things worse.

'I am *sorry*,' he'd say. 'I'm sorry I'm old and I'm sorry I'm ill.

I know it's terribly inconvenient. I know it makes your life *shit*.'

A day later, after a night's sleep, he resumed hostilities with re-doubled force – if I apologized. So now I just curled up with my phone and waited for him to get up and go to work. Only he didn't get up. I tried again to talk to him, but how desultory it sounded, I knew it did.

'I don't think you need to be too frightened, do you?' I said. 'You've been exercising, eating well. You look good. This must be the healthiest you've ever been.'

I reached for his hand and held it. He still didn't look at me.

'Do you see? Perhaps you don't…' he said.

'See what?'

'You say "healthy". Fine. I'm *not* healthy. Oh, no.'

'OK.'

'What I might explain to you,' he said, still looking away, 'is that I died when I had my heart attack. OK? When I was sitting there, waiting, I knew I was going to die, and I did die, and that's that. Now there is this lizardy part of me that *does* want to live, but it is just that, *that's* what's clinging on. Do you see? When you say you want your old nice Edwyn back, well, me too, but he's not here, do you understand? He never was here. What you met, or saw, or thought you saw, didn't exist and doesn't exist. Perhaps you can't understand. Why should you be able to? The fear I felt. I know what's coming now. And all there is is this…prehistoric, this disgusting…*will* – to live, to cling on! Even though my body aches from head to foot.'

'Look. I still think you're nice. You're still my nice Edwyn. And as I understood it, your last results were really encouraging. You've got the heart of a thirty-year-old...And a thirty-five-year-old.'

I tried to catch his eye to smile at him.

'So you're doing well. I'm sorry, I don't know what to say. Please don't be scared.'

His face darkened. He darted a look at me, and then resumed his staring at the ceiling. He pulled his hand away, started squeezing his fists, working his lips. His mouth was pleating and pursing. Again I reached to rub his hand, which was squeezing the other hand repeatedly. But he snatched it away and started scratching his cheek now, and kept scratching it.

'*Well?*' he said. 'I'm not *well*. I'm not *well!*'

Now he was scratching more rapidly. The scratching kept getting faster and more insistent, until with a breaking-free twist and a bolting jerk he was out of bed, and standing in the middle of the room, punching himself in the face. Then he rushed into the hallway, where there was a sudden cry and then a thump, followed by silence.

I went out there, and found him lying on his back, staring at the ceiling, and grinning, sort of, only with his mouth open. Like a baby in a cot. Next he started making an airy whining sound. I knelt down next to him, and smoothed out the wave of the pushed-up rug.

'What are you doing?'

'What's that?'

'Can you get up?'

'Oh dear! I must have fallen over!'

'Can you get up?'

'Don't know! Must have fallen over!'

He got up slowly. He came back into the bedroom slowly, taking each step with a shaky wonder, like he'd just stepped off a roller-coaster, or like he was a bleary old actress, making her way dazedly to the chat-show sofa. He sat down on the bed and I sat down next to him.

'What are you doing? You're frightening me.'

'What? Oh, no! I don't want to frighten you! Don't want to frighten my pusskins!'

Here he frowned terribly, and then he hugged me. He was hugging me hard but his hands were floppy and his expression looked cretinous and he was pursing his lips to kiss me. He kissed me all over my neck, as a child might a pet, or a favourite bear or doll: keeping an iron grip, and with 'kissy' noises: *mu-mu-mu*. At last I couldn't stand it and pulled away, and leant back away from him.

'Stop it. Why are you doing this? Are you in there?'

'What do you mean?'

'I'm frightened! What's happening? Edwyn? I'm worried you've got a brain tumour, or who knows what. Punching yourself.'

'Oh. Have I?' Now he took his floppy hands and started softly paddling at his scalp, 'Yes, I have got a brain tumour! See, you can feel it!' He nodded his head forward and tried to take my hand, to place on his head.

154

'Have you got any brain tumours? I bet you have! Let me feel. Let me feel! I bet you have!'

'Edwyn,' I said.

Finally I did manage to hold him still. Using all of my strength. He breathed into my shoulder.

My father died of the same thing that Edwyn had suffered. A myocardial infarction. One of the symptoms, described by people who've lived through it, is terrible fear, overwhelming anxiety. Was I really going to blame someone for being frightened?

In the nights after this latest upset, I tried, again, to think of a way forward. I could start again. If the sale of my father's house ever went through. I didn't want to. I thought of my mother, on the move. The energy for each flight, as for all of her lashing out, surely generated by the cowering cringe she lived in. Was I like that? Would I be? I'd hardly been unprone to impulsive moves. Dashes. Surges. The impetus seemed different, but perhaps it amounted to a similar insufficiency.

My father's sprees were both a reaction to and the cause of his confinement. It was his debts which meant he couldn't move from that house, even when the stairs got to be a daily torture. Was I too stupid – I couldn't be – to take a lesson from that? Could I trust myself? Not to make my life a lair.

Too often that wretchedness came into me. A torpor. A trance. I was in debt, once. Not for much – two hundred pounds or so – but once the third parties were involved, I soon learned what I was. And any idea that I could do something about it was lost. It's hard to account for now – this wilfulness – but I felt I just had to abide. Suffer through the vellications.

Those two years in Margaret's spare room, too: drinking all the time, my face growing strange to me.

6

How do I know what's coming? I always do know. Something around the eyes. Most recently, after a nice, peaceful month, when I told Edwyn I wasn't going to be in one Wednesday. There was that familiar little pause before he responded.

'Well, please don't get horribly drunk,' he said.

'I'm going to the pictures.'

'That's fine. I'm just asking, I'm just requesting, that you not get drunk. I'm not in the mood to clean up after you.'

'Clean up what?'

'I don't want to clean up your sick,' he said, thrusting his head forward, towards me.

Dinner was finished. There was just a dot of wine in his glass, and now he reached for the bottle to top up.

'Don't be nasty.'

'I'm not being nasty. It was just a request.'

'It is nasty. You're so sharp.'

'Well, that's how I talk, honey. I won't be done down for that. Just because I speak the King's English. Just because I didn't grow up in a *slum* in the *North*.'

'That's not what I mean.'

'I just don't want you to vomit all over the flat. Do you not think that's a reasonable request?'

'No. It's not a risk. You talk to me as if it's something I do all the time.'

'No, you don't do it all the time. If you did do it all the time, you wouldn't be living here, *I can assure you*.'

'I did it once, nearly two years ago. Once.'

'I know you don't do it regularly, I never said you did.'

'So you are being unfair.'

'No. I never said you'd done it again. I just don't *want* you to do it again.'

'There's no reason for you to think I might, though! It's not logical!'

'Well, it's not illogical, either. It's just fear. *You* gave me the fear. *OK?* I've never lived with anybody else whose vomit I had to clean up in every room. I still can't quite believe I *am* living with someone whose vomit I had to clean up in every room. Do you think that's *normal?*'

'Of course not. But nor was it normal what you did. I thought you were going to kill me.'

Edwyn shrugged, smirked, looked out of the window for a moment, with his chin up, his eyes narrowed.

'That's how you react to that, is it?' I said.

He turned back to me, still smirking.

'A lot of our hatred for one another comes from that night, doesn't it?' he said, staring at me. I didn't answer at first. I was doing what I used to do, I found, just sort of – drifting off, inside. It was hard to counter that.

'Do we hate each other?' I said, at last. 'I thought we loved each other. Last I heard.'

'Oh, *you* do. You hate me. You hate me with a *warm* hatred.'

'I don't know what you want. I got drunk. It happens to every-body. I'm sure when you were thirty-three or whatever I was...'

'*No.* I can *hold* my drink.'

'OK, but I'm sure there were times when you drank too much.'

'Of course there were, but I could *hold* it.'

'Were you holding it when you kicked down various doors? When you had the police called on you by your girlfriend? When you punched in that phone box? When you frightened your mother?'

He sighed.

'I was just *angry*. I didn't vomit all over people's houses and beds.'

'Great. OK.'

Now he stood, went into the kitchen. He came back with his whisky glass, half-filled that and sat down again.

'Christ, I'm sick of all this hatred and rancour. I've never had this in my life before. You had it all the time, you're used to it.'

'Have I? Go on.'

159

Here he spoke wearily, airily.

'Your *father*. You hated him, he was cruel to you, that's the only relationship you understand. A man being horrible to you and you being vicious back. So that's what you're recreating here. I am not your *father*. You don't have to go on being vicious. If you do go on being vicious, you're out. I don't want anything more to do with you. I'm not well and I can't take it. I won't spend my declining years fighting. If I do, there are things much more worth fighting for...'

'I didn't start a fight.'

'You don't have to see things like that. You don't have to see me as your *father* and this hateful man getting at you all the time. I'm just making *perfectly* ordinary, *perfectly* reasonable, *perfectly* ordinary human requests, why do you take it as such a *threat* to you, an attack on your "*self-respect*"? It isn't. It's just a human being asking the other human being who shares their fucking roof and bed to just, you know, remember that he exists, which I think a lot of the time you don't.'

'Of course I remember. And I didn't mention self-respect, where's that from?'

'I don't know what I am to you, but I don't *exist*. I'm not going to just *put up* with that, you know. With just being *obliterated*.'

'I'm not trying to do that.'

'To myself, now, I'm just this kind of fearful skivvy. I skivvy around and just go in fear of what you're going to get up to next.'

'That isn't a reaction to anything I do. "Get up to" – what does that mean?'

'Because you're so vicious to me. You're so sharp and defensive.'

'I'm not, Edwyn.'

Now he spoke through his teeth:

'You are, *Neve*.'

'No. I'm warm, attentive, mild. Rigorously so, in fact. Is that the problem? And I keep out of your way. You can't talk to me as if I'm someone who comes home and is sick here all the time, when I'm not. That's me being obliterated.'

'I was asking for reassurance. I'm not your *father*. He's the one who belittled you, all right? That's what I'm saying, I don't exist, you don't hear what I say, what you hear is your *father*.'

'All I did was tell you I was going to have a night out, let off steam.'

'The argument isn't about that. The argument is about your bizarre insistence that I'm attacking you just because I was asking for reassurance that you wouldn't come home and be sick everywhere. You read constantly, don't you? Has none of this ever made you consider, or allow, or admit, that people can represent something other than an opponent to you? That people can operate from motives other than wanting to harm *you* or laugh at *you* or belittle *you*?'

'Unless you're looking to hurt me, you know you don't need to ask for reassurance about my being sick. As I've said.'

'Well, the last time you "let off steam" that's what happened.'

By now my voice was very thin. Every word a moaning struggle. My body was clenched. Energy, will, draining away. But I couldn't give in.

'No, it's *not*. I've had plenty of nights out. I was happy that night. I just drank too much.'

'And forgot that I existed. And that this was where you were living, where you wanted to live, where *you* had said, *you*, that you wanted to live.'

'I had too much to drink, once.'

'Yes. And then I didn't exist. This just happened to be a convenient place for you to be sick in.'

'I'm sorry. Again. But this is what you think life is for, is it? This is what you think my life, my time, my energy, my goodwill is for? Conversations like this. I don't believe it.'

'Have you got any money at the moment, Neve?'

'Yes. Why?'

'Just an idea, that's all.'

'Right. I was waiting for that. Yes, I've got money. And more coming, of course. So. Go on.'

'Because your view of our living together, basically, is that I provide the circumstances in which you can be left alone to get on with your work, isn't it? And that's that. That's all right because that's the basis on which I took up with you. But I do expect just a minimum of acknowledgement of my existence from that. I know that you had faceless, nameless sources of that kind of support, grants, benefits, but I am not that. I've got a name and a face and a being. An existence of my own...'

'I have been working, and I may have been a bit absent...'

'Absence is fine. I wish you were more absent, all of the time.'

'Great. Shall we get a divorce, Edwyn?'

'I'd like you to need less attention from me.'

'I don't need attention, you do. I pay attention to you all the time, trying to head this sort of nonsense off.'

'Yes, but I don't *like* that. I don't *need* it or *want* it.'

'OK. So what do you want? No attention.'

'Attention as in, kiss me, love me, tell me you love me, pusskins – *that* I can live without. What I can't live without is somebody that I live with acknowledging that I'm here, that I have fears and hopes and worries of my own.'

'Of course I acknowledge that. I made a decision a while ago to stop asking you about yourself. It seemed like a habit. I didn't think it was bringing us closer. Do you want me to be disingenuous? These last few weeks I have been quieter because I'm trying to finish some work.'

'All I was asking for was a little automatic, tiny bit of reassurance, acknowledgement, recognition. I was worried about something. All you had to say was, Oh, for God's sake, don't worry, honey, it's fine, I'll be fine. But *no*.'

'If I'd said that, you just would have doubled down.'

'No, I wouldn't. That's all I was hoping for. Just a human reaction. What I get from you is your reaction to your *father*.'

'You know nothing about how he spoke to me.'

'Yes, I do. I know that he put you down.'

'You don't. You've never asked. He frightened me, but that wasn't the problem. The problem was that he existed, I'm afraid.'

'And the fact is that's all you respond to in me. You think that I'm putting you down. It's the only time I get a response. Otherwise, it's just pure demand, it's, Love me, tell me you love me.'

'I don't say that. I say, "I love you." That's what I say. And I do love you.'

'No. No, you only say that in order to be told it back. You know that. You know very well. And if you don't know that, then, you know, you need to go back to your therapist and she'll tell you that, if she isn't completely thick. You don't love me. You want to feel acknowledged and loved yourself.'

'So why are we married? Why can't we get divorced?'

'Well, I married you because I thought you wanted to be around me, and I thought you needed to be taken care of…I thought you needed to be supported and helped in life a bit, and that I could do that, I could offer that. I put it to you in just those terms, *if* you remember.'

Again. Did I? I suppose I did. So. Take that in.

'Not for love, then?' I said.

'Love as in?'

'I don't know. Chemistry. Attraction. Intimacy. Understanding.' He smirked, again.

'Well, those things are out of the window now, aren't they?'

'Right.'

'I said I'd take care of you. Some people might argue that taking care of someone was a loving thing to do. You, clearly, *don't* feel that way. I'm not asking for much because I know that I haven't got much to offer. All I can really offer is affection and a certain amount of support and, I hope, a bit of ease from care. I wanted to offer that. I want to offer that. Love for you is being welcome, isn't it, being wanted? I can offer you that. But I just expect in return somebody who acknowledges my existence and my own reality. Not someone who just thinks I'm a kind of pet that needs to be fed and patted. I know your need for affection is great and I'm willing to supply that. I haven't had any affection in my life either, I like the affection between us, but don't kid me that it's about love. It's about need for love. If you love someone, you don't want to frighten them or make them more worried than they have to be.'

'No. Of course not. I'm sorry. Won't you forgive me? For that one night.'

'No,' Edwyn said, frowning. 'I don't forgive you.'

'Right.'

'I don't forgive people.'

'No.'

I looked at his hands on the table then, by his plate, by his glass: swollen, crabbed. I looked at his face: worn out, defeated. He was blinking, as he did when he was upset.

The next morning, Edwyn had taken the day off work to go and see an exhibition, in town. It was a nice day, so I walked with him part of the way. We bought a coffee on Kensington High Street, then set off across the park. It was still misty at half past nine. A green and golden haze hung about the trees and on the damp grass large crows executed their leisurely inspecting strut. And here were squirrels, dashing. The crows lit on the fragments of lemon cake Edwyn was throwing. I held onto the elbow of his coat.

'Here comes Ted.'

'Craw craw,' said the crow.

'He looks like Douglas Bader.'

'Craw craw.'

We walked on, towards the pond, where we passed a man whose footwear caught Edwyn's attention.

'Oh, are they back in style? I used to love them. Dunlop Green Flashes. What a pleasure it was to get a nice pristine pair every summer.'

'When you were a boy?'

'Yes.'

'Did you wear them with little jeans and a stripy T-shirt?'

'Of course. Until it was time to change into my tennis gear. And then those Flashes would be covered in red dust from the court. It was dismaying after a few weeks how they'd turn pink from that dust…'

Edwyn used to live in town. In Marylebone, in a rich friend's spare room, when he first left university.

'You forget, don't you, that you had these other lives?' he said. 'That was *twenty years ago*. Twenty-*five* years. Gosh. And I was on this single bed, with this tiny old school desk to work at, just in a fog of Camel smoke all day long. I was quite keen on trying to cook back then. Trying to make myself useful, I suppose. But Christ, I must have stunk. How did I *taste* anything? I used to walk up every Saturday to the market and buy bags of vegetables, which would then proceed to collapse and rot within twenty-four hours. But I loved it, I kept going back!'

'Did you talk the lingo?'

'What's that?'

'I remember you talking the market trader's lingo, in the Portobello Road. "Two cukes, pound o' pots."'

'Oh, yes. Well, that's half the fun! And I'd remember who I could chat to, and go back to them the next week, for some chat and some friendliness. That's what you do in life, isn't it?'

At Marble Arch, we said goodbye. I stood and watched him go, head down, rushing. Oxford Street was so crowded. Edwyn hunched his shoulders, braced, dodged, and soon enough he disappeared.

ACKNOWLEDGEMENTS

The author would like to thank Arts Council England for a grant that enabled the writing of this book.

GWENDOLINE RILEY was born in London in 1979. She is the author of *First Love*, which was short-listed for the Women's Prize for Literature, the Dylan Thomas Prize, and the Gordon Burn Prize, and won the Geoffrey Faber Memorial Prize; and of *My Phantoms*, *Cold Water*, *Sick Notes*, *Joshua Spassky*, and *Opposed Positions*. She has also been awarded a Betty Trask Award and a Somerset Maugham Award, and has been short-listed for the John Llewellyn Rhys Prize. In 2018, *The Times Literary Supplement* named her as one of the twenty best British and Irish novelists working today.